DEADLY HALLUCINATION

Raider heard footsteps. He gripped the Colt. "Come down here, you—"

His eyes bulged when he saw it. A whitish shape gliding down the slope. And there was an Indian in full battle dress. The big man hesitated. What the hell was it? He squinted, trying to make it out. Was it a girl? And the Indian was right behind her. He wanted to fire the Colt but he wasn't sure what he was shooting at.

He was going to call out again but another voice echoed through the trees.

"Lawman. Look out!"

Raider was turning to run when the rifle exploded. He felt a pain in his head. Then everything went black. . . .

Other books in the RAIDER *series by*
J. D. HARDIN

RAIDER
SIXGUN CIRCUS
THE YUMA ROUNDUP
THE GUNS OF EL DORADO
THIRST FOR VENGEANCE
DEATH'S DEAL
VENGEANCE RIDE
CHEYENNE FRAUD
THE GULF PIRATES
TIMBER WAR
SILVER CITY AMBUSH
THE NORTHWEST RAILROAD WAR
THE MADMAN'S BLADE
WOLF CREEK FEUD
BAJA DIABLO
STAGECOACH RANSOM
RIVERBOAT GOLD
WILDERNESS MANHUNT
SINS OF THE GUNSLINGER
BLACK HILLS TRACKDOWN
GUNFIGHTER'S SHOWDOWN
THE ANDERSON VALLEY SHOOT-OUT
BADLANDS PATROL
THE YELLOWSTONE THIEVES
THE ARKANSAS HELLRIDER
BORDER WAR
THE EAST TEXAS DECEPTION
DEADLY AVENGERS
HIGHWAY OF DEATH

RAIDER

THE PINKERTON KILLERS

BERKLEY BOOKS, NEW YORK

THE PINKERTON KILLERS

A Berkley Book/published by arrangement with
the author

PRINTING HISTORY
Berkley edition/December 1989

ISBN: 0-425-11883-5

A BERKLEY BOOK ® TM 757, 375
Berkley Books are published by The Berkley Publishing Group,
200 Madison Avenue, New York, New York 10016.
The name "BERKLEY" and the "B" logo
are trademarks belonging to the Berkley Publishing Corporation.

PRINTED IN THE UNITED STATES OF AMERICA

10 9 8 7 6 5 4 3 2 1

This book is dedicated to
Randa Krise and Regina Cassidy

CHAPTER ONE

As Raider held the roan gelding on a steady southeast course, the big man in the saddle began to wonder for at least the hundredth time why he kept on in the service of that stern, bearded Scotsman named Allan Pinkerton. The wages weren't really good. But then again, the pay was better than that of a cowpoke or a stableman. Blacksmiths made more, but they had to stay in front of a forge all day, at least when they weren't pounding on an anvil. Cooks got fat, stagecoach drivers got sore backs, bartenders got red noses from nipping all the time. Even so, those lines of work would have seemed better to any sane man.

So why did he stay on?

Pinkerton just waited in Chicago, conspiring with that pain in the ass assistant of his, William Wagner. While they were warm in their cozy office, Raider was out in the field, braving the spring rain and mud under his slicker. His black Stetson hung limply over his rugged, grizzled face, ready to surrender to the water that fell from the sky. Underneath the slicker, the big man felt cold and damp. The loose, well-worn garment never quite kept him dry, even though it was better than nothing. His thick cotton shirt felt chilly against his skin, his denim pants were icy, his Justin boots were almost water-logged. If the Colt on his side had not been carefully wrapped in leather and oilcloth, it might have been just as soaked as the rest of him.

But a man had to take care of his guns. The rifle on Raider's sling ring was also wrapped in leather and oilcloth. Spring rain could ruin a Winchester. Raider wanted the rifle to be ready when he needed it.

The roan snorted, tossing its head.

Raider lifted his eyes, expecting to see the man he was chasing.

But there was nothing on the horizon.

He lowered his eyes until the gelding snorted again.

The big man from Arkansas reined up. "What is it, critter?"

Maybe the gelding smelled wet hay from the barn of some Missouri farmer. Raider was pretty sure he had crossed over into Missouri. Johnny Tipton was heading southeast, toward the Missouri River. Maybe the animal just smelled the river, although he couldn't be thirsty with all the rain that had been falling. Raider urged the roan forward.

"Might as well see what you're in a lather about."

He went back to thinking. At first, he considered the man he was after. Tipton had done some pretty bad things back in Fargo, North Dakota. Raider didn't really want to imagine the man's most heinous crime. It turned the big man's stomach, even though he had seen things that might be considered worse. Funny, how certain acts of wrongdoing just seemed sickening, when others didn't really provoke much reaction.

Raider wondered if he could catch Johnny Tipton, to put things right.

The big man sneezed. "Prob'ly gonna get the grippe," he muttered.

Why the hell did he stay on with Pinkerton? The tight-assed Scotsman and his assistant moved Raider around like a man on a checkerboard. They jumped him and crowned him and sent him straight into the pits of hell. The chicken-plucking jobs always went to Raider; cases that required the proper mixture of brains, brawn, and firepower. If the meanest bull got out of the corral, Pinkerton and Wagner sent Raider to catch it.

So why did he stay?

He considered the good points of his work. Nobody ever looked over his shoulder. Even if Pinkerton and Wagner bitched about him killing so many outlaws in his exploits, they always seemed to accept it. No, there was no real boss-man hollering at him, just those telegraph messages that told him where to go next, told him which new scalawag he had to chase.

Still, in spite of loving his freedom, the big man had other thoughts in the back of his mind. Somewhere in his imagination, he held a vision of a little horse farm near his home country in Arkansas. He never imagined farming because he hated that kind of work. No, he saw himself raising Standardbreds, going up to the fair in Little Rock once a year to compete with his neighbors. Sometimes the dream provided him with a woman, other times he just figured to have a few squaws around, preferably girls who did not speak English. It was easier to listen to a woman if you didn't rightly know what she was talking about. His dream made it easier to sleep in the saddle.

The roan snorted again, startling him awake.

"You're about the most fidgetty critter I ever—"

He lifted his eyes to see the broad river in front of him.

"The Missouri. Ever swam it afore, boy?"

The roan tossed his head back, rolling his eyes.

Raider wondered if maybe the animal was afraid of the water. He had seen it before. A horse that didn't like to swim could be a lot of trouble. And the river was swollen from spring rain.

"You better not drown me, honcho."

As he drew closer to the riverbank, Raider spotted the ferryman's line that stretched across the current. A small, wooden boat was being pulled toward the northern shore, coming straight for the big man. Maybe they wouldn't have to swim at all, not if the ferry was big enough.

Raider waited next to the roan, patting its neck. He decided to unwrap his Colt and ease it back into his holster before the boatman got there. Best not to take chances with a man he didn't know.

The boatman waved when he was close enough. "Howdy

partner," he called from the river. "Gonna cost you extra for the horse."

Raider drew back his slicker to reveal the Colt.

"Or maybe not," the boatman said.

"I'll pay whatever you charge," Raider replied. "Just get me on the other side o' the river."

The big man's black eyes made the ferryman nervous, but the short, fat captain managed to right his vessel on the bank. Raider and the gelding got in without too much fuss. The ferryman started to pull them across the swift, murky current.

"How much?" the tall Pinkerton asked.

The boatman licked his lips. "Two bits."

"That what you usually charge?"

"No, usually charge fifty cents."

Raider's quick hand produced a silver dollar.

"Give you change on the other side," the boatman offered.

Raider turned his rugged countenance to the other shore. "May not haveta give me change if you can give me information instead."

A frown from the fat sailor. "Hey, if you're the law—"

"I ain't."

"Whew. I was scared there. I'm operatin' this ferry without the permission of the Fort."

Raider looked at him. "Fort Osage?"

"That's the one."

He was west of Kansas City.

Would Johnny Tipton head for town?

The gelding spooked a little, prompting the big man to cover its eyes with a bandanna.

"Nice trick," the boatman said. "Have to remember that one."

Raider glared at the captain, piercing the little man's face with his black irises. "How many men you took across this week?"

"Ten, maybe. Hey, it ain't a easy life neither. I—"

"Save it for the preacher," the big man rejoined. "You see a boy 'bout thirty years old, stocky, scar on his right cheek, dresses like a farmer?"

"Hmm, I ain't sure."

"Has a beard," Raider continued. "Low brow. Ridin' a mule mebbe."

The ferryman gave a loud guffaw. "Now that mule I remember. Hell, I don't know what that boy had been feedin' it, but that danged critter dropped enough shit in my boat to sink it, I tell you."

"The man," Raider insisted. "Did he have a scar on his right cheek?"

"A beaut, yessiree. Long and ugly. Yep, I didn't recall him until you said about that mule. Come to think of it, that one did look pretty mean. Is he in some kind of trouble?"

Raider nodded, turning back toward the shore. "He will be if I catch up t' him. I don't reckon he said which way he was goin'?"

"Do I get to keep the change if I know?" the ferryman asked.

"You earned that already, honcho. Figure on another two bits if you can point me in the right direction."

The boatman pointed west. "Asked me about the steamer boat into Kansas City. I didn't see him catch it, but he hung around on the other side for a while. On one of my runs the next mornin', I noticed he was gone. That was day before yesterday."

"Had the steamer gone through?"

The fat captain shrugged. "Can't rightly say. I sleep like a sturgeon at night. Don't even hear the whistle when it comes through."

It made sense to Raider that Tipton would run to Kansas City. He had been on the trail for a long time, all the way from Fargo. Stolen money was hot in his pockets. A man could have a good time in K.C., especially if he was well-heeled.

"What'd this boy do wrong?" the boatman asked.

"Stole some. An' other stuff."

"What kind of other stuff?"

Raider's stomach turned. "I don't wanna talk 'bout it."

"Hmm. That bad. You a marshal?"

"Pinkerton."

The ferryman laughed. "Never could figure out why a man would want to do that line of work."

Raider knew finally, from the old feeling that came around

every time he got back on a fresh trail. He liked chasing outlaws, just to see if he could catch them. It was a game, sponsored by Pinkerton and Wagner. Raider wore the crown, a checker piece ready to jump. And when the big man from Arkansas caught up to Johnny Tipton, he planned to jump all over him.

CHAPTER TWO

A cold, spring drizzle hung over Chicago, prompting William Wagner to light the wood stove that stood in the center of the Pinkerton offices. Normally one of the clerks or a messenger boy tended the stove, but on this particularly miserable day, Wagner stoked it himself. He wanted to stay busy, to keep his mind off the other dreaded task that he had to perform around noontime.

A door rattled behind him.

Wagner gazed back to see the broad figure of Allan Pinkerton standing in the doorway of his private office. "Has he come yet?" Pinkerton asked.

Wagner shook his head. "Another half hour, sir."

Pinkerton grunted and turned back into his office.

Wagner stared into the flames for a moment before he closed the door of the wood stove. He ambled about the office for a while, poking his face into everything, disturbing his staff with the good intentions of a nosy boss. Finally he realized what he was doing and returned to his desk to wait out the last few minutes before the dreaded appointment.

Pinkerton came into the doorway again. "Not here, yet?"

Wagner shook his head.

"You know, William, it's not every day that we receive a

territorial marshal. These men can be crude, rough."

Wagner shrugged. "Yes, I know. But he is from Minnesota after all. I hear that it's not nearly as rough there as it once was."

Pinkerton grunted, but motioned to his assistant. "Come on, William. How about a cup of coffee?"

The pot was steaming on the potbellied stove in Pinkerton's office.

Wagner took a hot cup and sat down opposite Pinkerton's huge, oak desk. "Looks like the rain is going to drown us."

"Raider!" Pinkerton said suddenly. "Why is he always making trouble? Why can't he leave well enough alone?"

"He only killed twelve people," Wagner replied. "And as far as I can see, they all needed it. We have his report."

Pinkerton held up a brown, stained piece of paper. "Aye. Would you like to hear it again?"

Wagner lowered his eyes, trying not to smile.

"Listen, William: 'I done stopped them boys that was shootin' up all them them sodbusters out here in Minnesota.' Poignant."

"He did stop the trouble, sir."

Pinkerton sighed deeply. "I know, lad, I know. But you saw the clippin' from that paper. It came with the marshal's request to see us personally. He didn't forward his remittance either."

"Could be that he's trying to weasel out of paying us our fee," Wagner offered. "I mean, if he's—"

"He'd never do that, gentlemen! Not in the name of the great state of Minnesota!"

Wagner turned back to see a tall, redheaded man standing in the doorway. He was dressed in a fresh, black suit and held a narrow-brimmed Stetson in his hands. A rugged face sported a bushy, red mustache that did not move even when the marshal talked.

"Mr. Johnson," Pinkerton said, standing behind his desk. "Won't you come in and have a seat. Would you like some coffee? William?"

Wagner started to get up.

Marshal Johnson regarded him with piercing blue eyes. "No need," he said sternly. "I just came to have my say."

Wagner felt a sinking feeling in his gut. It was finally going to happen, he thought. A state agency was going to bring a suit against Pinkerton. All because of Raider's reckless gun hand. The petulant Scotsman would surely discharge the tall brute from Arkansas.

"Did you get my letter?" Johnson asked.

Pinkerton nodded. "Yes, sir. And just let me say, I want to offer my apologies for our agent. Raider will no longer be in our employment after today. I'll see to it that—"

"Fire him?" Johnson exclaimed. "You must be daft."

Wagner stared at the lawman. "But we thought you had come here to complain about Raider."

Johnson sighed dejectedly, leaning back in his chair. "I'm supposed to. We got this new governor that's promisin' to stop all the roughhousin' that we had for a while. He's the one who sent me."

Wagner smiled a little more. "And you don't agree with him?"

"Hah!" Johnson exclaimed. "The only way to deal with lawless scum like the Quinn brothers is to shoot their asses off!"

Pinkerton laughed involuntarily.

Johnson blushed. "Sorry for the language."

"No offense taken," Pinkerton replied.

"Why do you think I hired your man in the first place?" Johnson offered. "The governor wants me and my deputies to stop carryin' guns. Can you believe it? Says we won't need them to keep the peace."

"Rather ridiculous, I'd say," Wagner chimed in.

Johnson nodded, squinting like he wasn't sure what *ridiculous* meant. "I'm supposed to complain," the marshal said. "To tell you that we won't pay your fee. But I can't do that. Not after what Raider did for us. I wish I could have hired him. Did he tell you I offered to make him a deputy?"

"No," Wagner replied drily, "he neglected to mention that."

Johnson started to dig into his pocket. "I know I'm not supposed to pay you, but I took up a collection before I left. Some of it came from the sodbusters that your man helped, the rest of it came from me and my deputies. Eighty-five dollars. It's all I could scrape up."

Johnson put a leather pouch on Pinkerton's desk.

"How long did it take Raider to round up the Quinn gang?" Wagner asked.

"Six days," Johnson replied. "He brought 'em all in on a buckboard. Said he had to kill 'em a couple at a time because they didn't want to come in to stand trial. I tell you, he saved the state of Minnesota a lot of bother. I never seen anythin' like it."

Pinkerton opened the leather pouch and took out five dollars. "Here. You've overpaid us. Have dinner tonight at one of the finer hotels."

Johnson took the five, but shook his head. "I'll just take this back to the widow lady. She really couldn't afford to part with it, but she seemed to take to Raider pretty much."

"This widow," Wagner said, "was she old and ugly?"

"No, young and pretty," Johnson replied.

Pinkerton cleared his throat. "That will be enough, William. Now, Marshal Johnson, I suggest that you stay at my house tonight, as my guest. I insist on it, in fact."

"All right," Johnson said reluctantly. "But there's a train back to St. Paul day after tomorrow. I have to be going then."

They all shook hands and Wagner dispatched one of the office boys to escort Johnson through the rain to Pinkerton's home.

Wagner smiled at his boss. "I wonder what Raider carries for a good luck piece?"

"I'll bet he's part Irishman," Pinkerton replied. "At least we don't have to fire him. Where is he anyway?"

"In the Dakotas, or that was where he was a month or so ago. Who knows where he is now?"

"Well, we'll be hearin' from him soon enough. But now that this business is over, we have work to do, William."

Wagner returned to his desk, feeling as if a burden had been lifted. He went through his papers with a newfound zest, at least until the messenger boy arrived. The lad wore a doleful expression.

"Any word from Idaho?" Wagner asked, glaring at the boy.

The kid shook his head. "No, sir. Just these."

Wagner tossed them aside. "This isn't good."

"No, sir."

"That will be all."

"May I leave for the day, sir?"

Wagner sighed. "Yes, yes. I'll send one of the others to wait at Western Union."

The lad scampered away from Wagner's desk.

Wagner's morning cheer had departed, leaving behind the same gray drizzle with which he had started the day.

He had to go in and tell Pinkerton. There was no way around it. Damn that Stanton. Wagner had given him direct orders to wire back at least once a week. The wires had come three times, but then had stopped.

He explained it all to his boss.

Pinkerton rubbed his thick beard. "You're just bringin' this to me now, William!"

"I sent the first three men to Idaho just as I would for any other case. Nothing special, mind you. This miner's daughter had disappeared."

"So have four of our agents!" Pinkerton cried. "Damn it, man, why didn't you say something to me?"

Wagner lowered his head. "I sent McGovern to look into it first. Then, when he didn't come back and I didn't hear from him for a month, I sent Walters. Finally, when Walters failed to report back, I sent Eagleton."

"And he never came back," Pinkerton accused. "So that's when you sent Stanton to look for the first three."

Wagner sighed. "I made a mistake. But this business with Raider had me distracted. It seemed as though I was following policy."

"You were," Pinkerton replied. "You were. Four of our men missing."

"We haven't confirmed that yet," Wagner replied. "After all, we go long stretches without hearing from our men. It's not that unusual. Look at Raider, I haven't heard from him in a month either."

"Yes," Pinkerton snapped, "but with Raider, you don't worry about him. You worry about who he's killing."

"Well, I suppose that's—"

Pinkerton shot him a glaring look. "Since you've bungled this, William, I'm leavin' it to you to straighten it out."

"Yes, sir."

"And what do you plan to do?"

"I'll send Raider to Idaho," Wagner replied. "As soon as I hear from him."

Pinkerton leaned back, nodding. "At last you decide to do the right thing."

Wagner tensed, wondering how long it would take to get the big man from Arkansas on the job.

CHAPTER THREE

Things had not worked out the way Raider had planned. Like the man he was chasing, Raider had caught the steamer near Fort Osage. A big, white boat named *Queen of the Missouri* took him and the roan to Kansas City, arriving before the big man was able to catch a nap on a couple of bales of Louisiana cotton. Somehow, it didn't seem right to Raider, traveling so far so fast, riding along with goods that had come thousands of miles to market in Kansas City. It seemed unnatural.

The trip was so short that he barely had time to ask about Johnny Tipton. But nobody remembered the outlaw. Maybe it wasn't the same steamer. And then again, maybe things just weren't going to pan out. He felt like a dog that had picked up a trail, only to have a wide creek snuff out the scent.

Still, he was hopeful for a while, at least until he went to stable his mount. The livery was full. A trail drive had just rolled in from the south and a couple hundred cowboys were having a riot. Most of them were sleeping with their horses because they couldn't afford a good hotel.

So Raider decided to go top-dollar for a while. Usually the big man checked into a cheap boardinghouse or a friendly bordello. But he didn't feel like fooling with it. He was tired and worn and hungry, prompting him to frequent one of

K.C.'s finer establishments, a hotel called the Royal House.

The man at the desk winced noticeably when Raider walked in.

"I beg your pardon, sir," the snippy clerk said in a indignant voice. "We aren't taking any cowboys just—"

"It ain't polite to beg," Raider replied. "Besides, I ain't no cowboy. I'm a Pinkerton agent an' I got a whole slew o' back pay in my pocket. What's your goin' price for a room?"

The clerk stiffened proudly. "Our cheapest room is three dollars a day."

Raider produced a double eagle from his pocket. "Then gimme one for five dollars a day, boy. Write me up for four days. Here's another ten in scrip for food. Which way t' the kitchen?"

The clerk looked sick as he eyed the money. Raider wasn't exactly telling him the truth about his back pay. He had just parted with his last thirty dollars, but he didn't have to tell the clerk that. And there was still the roan to contend with. He had to stable the animal after it had carried him so far in search of Johnny Tipton.

"You got a stable hereabouts?" Raider asked.

"Yes," the clerk replied, still reluctant to give in to Raider's wishes. "But it will cost—"

"I don't give a gopher's ass what it costs, honcho. There's a roan out front what needs oats an' water. I'd be much obliged if you'd take care of it for me, Jasper."

"I don't think I can—"

Raider grinned at him. "Well, maybe your boss can take care of it for me. I mean, I'd hate to have to tell him you couldn't handle it. Might make you look bad an' I ain't one for gripin'. Course, my roan is the one who might complain. You hear me, Jasper?"

"My name isn't Jasper," replied the red-faced clerk.

"How 'bout a key for my room?"

The key hit the counter with a sharp click.

Raider picked it up, pointing it at the blushing man. "Now you see here, Zeke. It don't take much t' be nice t' folks. Now, if you'll just write me out a receipt—"

After a bath and a hot steak, Raider slept through until morning. But he opened his eyes at daybreak, aware that he had not caught Johnny Tipton. It wouldn't be easy, not with all the cowboys in town. Tipton would hardly stand out in the crowd. Still, Raider figured he could catch him if he put all his resoures to work.

He went downstairs to have breakfast but the dining room wasn't open. In the kitchen, he managed to talk the cook into a plate of steak and eggs. Breakfast tasted good, but as it happened, it would be the last thing that went right, at least for a while.

At the end of his fourth day in Kansas City, Raider felt worse than when he had arrived. It appeared that every possible barrier had come between him and Johnny Tipton. Many times in his career, Raider felt like he would not be able to catch a fugitive from the law. But this was the first time he had actually believed that Johnny Tipton might be gone for good. Raider wondered how real lawmen felt when an outlaw escaped their jurisdiction. Some sheriffs or marshals might have said good riddance to a criminal who rode away, never to be seen again. Others might have followed for a while, giving up when the going got tough. And there was probably that one-in-a-hundred lawman who stayed on the trail until his heart just sank.

Raider wondered if he was going to feel as bad when word got around the agency that he had let a man get away. The big man knew in his heart that there was no real excuse for letting Tipton slip through his grasp. Not that a few things hadn't arisen to impede his investigation.

A second wave of cowboys had ridden into Kansas City to join the first bunch. Now there were twice as many rough-and-tumble cowpokes for Tipton to hide among. Who could respond to a description of the outlaw when there were a hundred like him at every turn?

Wagner's telegram hadn't helped either. It came the third day, after Raider had requested his back pay. "Don't leave Kansas City," the message read. "Back pay will follow shortly. Advise Western Union of your whereabouts."

No back pay. That meant Wagner really didn't want him to leave Kansas City. It also meant that somebody was probably on the way to see Raider. Maybe Stokes or Stanton. Probably coming with hateful news about some bastard sidewinder that nobody else could catch.

But what about Johnny Tipton? Raider had to find him. It was a matter of pride. Besides, what else did he have to do? He couldn't whore or gamble, not with empty pockets. All he could do was search the back alleys and streets, looking for a stocky man with a beard, a thick ape who had killed and robbed and done other things that Raider didn't like to think about.

On the evening of his fifth day in Kansas City, Raider slipped out past the suspicious desk clerk who was undoubtedly getting ready to ask for more money. Raider had sifted through his belongings to find a couple of two-bit pieces and some nickels and dimes, enough money to at least have a few drinks in a cheap saloon. Best to have them now, before his livery and his hotel bills came due. Why the hell hadn't Wagner sent his back pay?

He decided not to think about it.

Instead, he stole out into the streets, hoping that by some miracle of luck he might be able to find Johnny Tipton before Wagner dealt him the next assignment. Maybe he would look across a crowded barroom and see that bearded face staring back at him. It had happened before. And it would happen again, only nothing would go Raider's way when it finally did.

Some things in life just couldn't be explained, Raider thought.

Take the Kansas City whores, for instance. If Raider had been possessed of a full wallet, there wouldn't have been a willing whore within a mile of him. He would have searched, only to come up empty. But now, when he had spent his last dime on a mug of bad homemade beer, the girls were everywhere, begging him to lie down with them.

"These cowboys are so cheap," said one thick-lipped lass. "I'll do it for four bits, honey. Hey, come on!"

Raider just had to walk on by her.

The pattern remained the same. Hit the dives, look for Tipton or any man who might be him. Listen until somebody called his name. No Johnny, no luck.

So he drank up the last of his change and started back to the hotel. He'd have to send another wire to Wagner. The man in Chicago would have to come through with some back pay. He couldn't leave Raider hanging.

"Hey, cowpoke. You willin'?"

Raider lifted his eyes. "Rosey?"

She squinted back at him. "Raider? Son of a gun. Come on over here and talk at me a spell. This town has been drier than a popcorn fart, at least while these cowboys has been here."

The big man sauntered over into the shadows. Rosey looked a little older, but she still cut a fine figure of a woman. She had been one of his favorites until she had just up and disappeared.

"Rosey, what the devil are you doin' out in this alley?"

She sighed, her bosom heaving up and down. "Raider, I just plain fell on hard times. You remember the house I had, out in Liberty?"

Raider tipped back his Stetson. "Do I? Clean sheets an' a big wooden tub. Hell, I come lookin' for you a few years ago but the house was some kind o' boardin' school."

"Come lookin', huh? You and every other saddle tramp. Damn it all, this town is gettin' too respectable when a girl like me has to take to the back alleys. In my good days, I had twenty girls workin' for me. I stopped layin' down, except for a few men, like you. Hey, whatever happened to that old partner of yours?"

"Aw, he got married and moved back east."

Rosey grimaced. "Marriage. That's what sunk me. I hitched up with this good-lookin' feller from Nebraska. Had big dreams, he did. Thought we'd move out there, become landed gentry."

"What's landed gentry?"

"Aw, never mind, Raider. You always was a thick head. Anyways, all that farm boy wanted to do was spend my money. Turns out he didn't even own that farm we was livin' on."

"Tough, huh."

She smiled. "No, not like you think. My big problem was tryin' to be somethin' I wasn't. I should have stayed whorin' to begin with. Had me all them girls in that fine house. I sold it for beans. Never should have listened to that boy. He was pretty though. And he had what it took to make a woman happy, between the legs, I mean."

Raider felt an urge hearing such talk. But he didn't have a penny to his name. That didn't make him stop wanting it, though.

"Say, Raider," Rosey started, "as I recall, you had enough down there to bring tears to a girl's eyes. How about it?"

"Aw, Rosey, I'm so broke I cain't pay attention."

A deep sigh from the evening lady. "Nothin', huh?"

"I could owe you."

"Don't worry about it," she replied. "I'm kinda in the mood anyway. Seein' you has brought back some of the good memories, let's do it for old time's sake."

Raider didn't have any objections. He told her that he would be good for five dollars when his back pay came in. Rosey said that would be fine with her. She took his hand and led him down a long, dark hallway.

CHAPTER FOUR

When they reached Rosey's small bedroom, she took off Raider's Stetson and flung it on the seedy mattress.

Raider immediately grabbed his hat and hung it on the wall. "Ain't takin' no chances, honey. Not the way things have been runnin' for me."

Rosey's rouged cheeks lifted as she smiled. "Still superstitious, huh? Why don't you cowboys ever change?"

"Hat on the bed is bad luck," the big man replied. "Besides, I ain't no cowboy."

"And I ain't no whore," she said, chortling.

Raider gestured around the dim room. "You ain't doin' so well, are you, Rosey?"

He hadn't meant the remark to hurt her, but he saw her face slacken. She looked away from him, sighing. Raider felt like hell.

"Hey, I'm sorry, honey—"

Her head flew up, her neck stiffened proudly, her shoulders straightened. "It's been a long time since Liberty," she replied. "This is the best I could do. I share the hallway with a couple of other girls. You'll hear 'em coming and going."

"Hey, Rosey, I didn't mean nothin'—"

"Oh, you just said it because I called you a cowboy. I shoulda remembered that you're a high-falutin Pinkerton detective. I—oh, Raider—"

Naturally she started to cry. And just as naturally, the big man could not stand up to female tears. He curled his arms around her and gave her a gentle bear hug.

"I always put the stirrup in my mouth," he whispered.

She sobbed on his chest. He could smell her faint perfume. She was still firm after all those years on her back.

"We don't have to do it," he told her. "I can just sit here with you for a while."

She seemed to catch her breath. "No."

"You want me to leave?"

"No."

"Well, what d' you want, honey?"

"I want to do it," she replied. "I'm all wet. Cryin' always makes me that way. I want it."

He felt her hand creeping down to his crotch. It didn't take much for her to get him started. After a couple of minutes, Rosey had to unbutton his pants. Raider's prick sprang free from his tight jeans. Rosey's hot hand closed around the thick base of his shaft.

"Damn me if it's not bigger than I remember," she said softly.

Raider touched her shoulders. "Maybe we oughta lay down."

Rosey smiled at him, rolling her eyes. "Mind if I get on my knees first?"

He grimaced at her. "You never went in for that Frenchy stuff."

She shrugged. "An old girl has to learn new tricks. Why don't you let me show you?"

Before he could protest, Rosey dropped down to the floor. He heard something clicking and then he felt her lips on his cock. Her mouth didn't seem right, not like the way he had known it with other women. She began to slide hotly over his prick, taking him in and out between her thick lips.

"Rosey—"

He had never felt anything like it.

"Honey—"

So soft and wet and quick.

"Girl—"

Like she didn't have any teeth.

Raider exploded inside her mouth. Rosey seemed to gag a little but she stayed on him, draining everything he had to offer. When he was dry, she stood up, still keeping one hand on his cock. The other hand popped something back into her mouth.

"False teeth?" Raider asked.

She grinned and he could not tell in the dim light. "You'll never know. How was it?"

Raider just grunted. He didn't want to talk about it. Rosey kept pulling on him, trying to keep him rigid.

"Don't want you to die before I've had mine," Rosey said.

Raider pushed her hand away. "When'd you ever know me not t' have enough t' keep a woman happy? Let's get nekkid."

Raider watched her as she took off her clothes. She was big, the way he liked them. Skinny women didn't have anything to hang on to. When she was completely nude, he lowered his lips to her large, brown nipples.

"Umm," she said as he suckled, "that feels good. When are you gonna take off your clothes?"

"I thought you might take 'em off for me."

She helped him with his boots and then his shirt. When she had his pants off, she fell on him, rubbing her breasts on his prick. Raider sprang to life in a hurry.

"You have learned some tricks," he said.

"Lie back and watch," she offered. "I'll fuck your damned brains out."

Raider stretched out on the lumpy mattress. Rosey straddled him, guiding the head of his prick on her wet cunt. She took him in with one quick motion, sitting down on his massive length. Her face contorted into an expression of unexpected pleasure. She yelped like a dog, making Raider wonder if her throaty bursts would disturb the other whores. The bed started to bang against the wall to add to the noise of lovemaking.

She rode him for a long time, gasping for air, grinding with desperate thrusts of her hips. "Come, you cowboy bastard," she said through clenched teeth. "Come before I—ohh—"

She was getting dry.

Raider shifted, grabbing her shoulders, pulling her around until she was beneath him. "Easy there," he whispered, smiling. "You're gonna get what you want."

"Let me put my legs on your shoulders," she offered. "I want it as deep as you can get it. My old sweet potato has seen a lot of whangers. I want you to butter it for me real good."

When her legs were in place, Raider began to rock the bed again. Rosey seemed to get wetter with each thrust. She hung on, trying to extract his release. The big man seemed to be tireless.

"Come, damn it," she said. "Shoot!"

Raider just kept pounding away, driving his shaft in and out of her.

Rosey reached down between her legs, gripping the lips of her cunt. She tightened her flesh around him, prompting his prick to swell. Raider collapsed with his release. Rosey screeched in his ear, yelping again as she found her own climax.

"Damn," she moaned finally, "I ain't had it like that in a long time."

Raider rolled off her, lying beside her on the mattress. "Well, honey, your ol' Arkansas crawdaddy still has a few drops left in him."

She snuggled against his chest, rubbing his stomach. "I'm savin' my money," she said unexpectedly. "I'd like to get back to Liberty. There's a little house over there that I can get for a couple of hundred dollars. It's not much, but I could fix it up and plant a garden."

Raider closed his eyes, hoping she wasn't in a mood to talk. Sometimes women liked to talk in bed. It was almost a surefire way to ruin things.

"Seems funny, seein' you without your gun."—She was in the mood.—"I'm kinda glad K.C. passed that law, that you can't carry guns anymore. Plenty still carry 'em, though, hidden I mean. Hey, your boot felt kind of heavy—"

Raider wondered if he was going to have to top her again to get her to shut up. Sometimes it was the only way. He sure would have enjoyed a nap. But he would never get to sleep with her talking.

"Yeah, we used to have some pretty good shoot-outs in

Liberty. Those were the days. You'd never know the place now. Hell, you couldn't have been more than twenty back then. Did you—"

He reached for her hand, to guide it back to his prick.

Rosey sighed deeply, like she appreciated the gesture. "I can suck it again," she said.

She couldn't talk with it in her mouth.

Rosey was going down as the woman screamed.

Raider sat up, reaching for his boots.

"It's nothing," Rosey insisted. "One of the other girls has a new boyfriend. She wants to get hitched, but he won't. She says she's gonna keep whorin' until he does. He says he wants her to quit but he won't marry her."

Raider hesitated. "Just a lover's quarrel, huh?"

Rosey nodded. "Now, let me—"

The girl screamed again: "Damn you, damn you. How am I supposed to make a living if you don't support me?"

A man's voice came lower behind the woman's. "Honey, don't—" He trailed off.

Rosey was listening as intently as Raider.

"What's his name?" the big man asked.

"I don't know, Jimmy, Johnny, something like that."

Raider's hand touched his boot. "Johnny Tipton?"

"I don't know."

The quarrel seemed to die down.

Rosey looked up at the big man. "What have you got in that boot?"

Raider shrugged. "Just a little protection. Nothin' for you t' git excited about. I'm chasin' this boy, that's all."

"You're always chasin' somebody." She sighed again. "You know, if the sheriff catches you with that pistol in your boot, he'll lock you up for sure."

"Mebbe," the big man replied. "But like you say, a lotta men still carry their iron hidden. Besides, I reckon I got some rights. I am a Pinkerton, you know. That oughta count for somethin'."

She touched his limp cock. "Looks like you ain't in the mood anymore. Let's just talk."

Raider pushed her head toward his prick. "You can get me in the mood, if you—"

But the girl started shouting again. Raider tensed when he heard what she was saying. It echoed loud and clear through the night air.

"Damn you," she was yelling. "Damn you, Johnny Tipton."

CHAPTER FIVE

Will Stanton was a good Pinkerton agent. In the hierarchy of his colleagues, he was considered near the top, surpassed only by Henry Stokes, Ben Morton, and the former detective, Doc Weatherbee. Stanton was considered by most to be better than Raider. Not tougher, but almost as tough. A little smarter than the big man from Arkansas, although Stanton considered Raider's raw instincts to be superior to his own. Not as good with a Colt, but a little better than Raider with a Winchester. Stanton didn't even carry a sidearm, except when he was close to catching an adversary.

Pinkerton and Wagner found Stanton to be close to their image of what the ideal agent should be: controlled, thinking, forceful when necessary but restrained in the general tone of an investigation. Unlike Raider, Stanton never left a trail of bodies to mark his way. Stanton hadn't really killed anyone in a couple of years. He always seemed to find a way to avoid it.

Stanton usually did as he was told by Wagner. When Wagner said to check in every week, Stanton did it. That was what had brought him down from the mountains, into the low forests to the north of Idaho Springs. He knew for sure that there was a wire at the Springs, but he wasn't sure how Wagner would react to his being more than two weeks late. It was the first time Stanton had not followed procedure.

The rangy, blond-haired, brown-eyed Stanton had camped above a precipice on a ledge that overlooked what he thought must be the Snake River. He could see a faint twinkle of light on the horizon, although he could not be sure if it was the town or simply a lone miner's lantern burning brightly at a shorter distance. He'd have to wait until tomorrow.

Stanton wrapped a blanket around his shoulders, huddling near the fire at about the same time Raider was reaching for his Colt. Stanton felt uneasy, probably because he did not have much to report to Wagner. No clue as to the whereabouts of the missing girl, or of the other agents who had preceded him.

He shivered against the night wind, gazing back up at the stand of trees that rose along the line of a gentle slope.

His mount snorted.

Stanton looked at the animal, which was the main reason he had stopped to rest. The chestnut mare had seemed like she was ready to drop underneath him before. Now she seemed feisty enough.

Standing, the whippet-thin agent brought up his rifle. He could not hear any movement in the trees. The breeze was too strong; the boughs were creaking, the leaves fluttered like hummingbird wings.

"Who is it?" Stanton called.

Nothing.

He sat by the fire again.

His investigation had not been entirely fruitless. He had managed to turn up a couple of rummies who explained the girl's disappearance. An Indian spirit had taken her, a Blackfoot shaman who always came back for a bride in the spring. Girls had disappeared that way before, one man swore over a mug of beer. Another claimed to have seen the Blackfoot ghost himself, which Stanton did not doubt, given the man's consumption of alcohol.

Will Stanton was a smart man. He had never believed in such things. Had he seen something like that with his own eyes, a spirit or such, he would have believed it. Of course, sitting in the mountains on a moonless night made a man wonder.

A wolf howled somewhere nearby.

Stanton felt a rush through his body. The howling had not scared him so much as the suddenness of the sound reverberating over the wind. Wolves would not bother him, not as long as he had the fire.

The chestnut startled again.

Stanton gazed over his shoulder, telling the animal in a cautious voice: "Never you mind, dobbin. They ain't gonna eat you. Not as long as I got old Chester here."

He patted the rifle underneath his blanket, more to convince himself than to convince the horse.

The wind died a little but the animal continued to spook.

Stanton wondered if the wolves were getting closer. He threw two more logs on the fire, watching the flames rise higher. The howling seemed farther away. Stanton considered the possibility of Indians, but decided that they were too scattered this far north to make any trouble.

As he was settling into his blanket again, the footsteps came through the trees. The trodding was noisy, deliberate. Stanton stood up, dropping the blanket from his shoulders, lifting the Winchester.

The chestnut mare began to buck and whinny.

Stanton lowered his rifle when he saw the shape as it came into the light of the fire. He started to say something, but a weapon exploded somewhere behind him. The bullet caught him on the right side, sending him to the ground where he died, twitching violently until the end.

Another figure joined the first intruder.

"Mister Pinkerton has one less agent."

"They just won't learn."

"Bury him with the others."

"I wonder if he's going to send more?"

"Just bury him. It will all be over soon."

"I hope you're right."

The wind picked up again as they loaded the body of Will Stanton on the back of the chestnut mare.

CHAPTER SIX

Raider had troubles of his own.

Down the hall, the girl was still screaming. "I shoulda run away from you the minute I saw you, Johnny Tipton."

Raider eased the Colt out of his boot. It was the only way he could carry it now that sidearms were no longer allowed in Kansas City. He thumbed back the hammer and stayed still, listening. Maybe Johnny Tipton would walk right by him when he went for the door. Or maybe he would try to talk the girl into letting him share her bed for the night. Either way, the big man had to take him.

Rosey got off the bed, sliding next to him. "Raider, I—"

He held up a hand and shook his head. Rosey backed away. The gun scared her. After all her years of dealing with gun-happy cowboys and drifters, the cold glint of iron still made her nervous.

Down the hall, the girl was whimpering. The sobs became muffled, like she had put her head into Johnny Tipton's chest. He was going to remain with her. Damn weak-willed woman, Raider thought. Now he would have to take Tipton straight on instead of reaching out into the hall to grab him by the scruff of the neck.

Resting his gun on the bed, he pulled on his pants and

boots. Rosey handed him his shirt and his Stetson. Raider kissed her lightly on the cheek and then picked up the Colt.

"Be careful," she whispered. "I didn't like the looks of that one."

Raider's heart mule-kicked the hollow of his chest. Tipton would have a gun or some kind of weapon. He was not the kind to obey any law.

"What room?"

Rosey held up two fingers. "Second door down."

Slipping into the hall, Raider felt his way in the shadows. He stopped by the second door and listened. The bed was creaking. Johnny Tipton had climbed into the saddle.

Raider rested his back against the wall, tensing, taking a deep breath. He wondered if the door was too strong. A man could break his leg trying to smash in a thick, oak door. The big man couldn't remember if there were any oak trees in Missouri.

One application of his Justin boot splintered the door.

Raider lowered the Colt at the man in the bed. "Don't flinch, Johnny, or I'll—"

Tipton looked up, his face flashing in the light of a candle. His beard had vanished, his hair was cut short. He looked to be skinnier than the description Raider had been given. The big man never would have found him, even if he had come face to face with the outlaw.

Tipton tried to smile. "Hey, hoss, you got the wrong man. I ain't the man you want. I ain't Johnny Tipton."

Raider gestured toward the girl. "She called your name."

Tipton scowled, slapping the woman. "Stupid bitch."

"Get out from under him," Raider told her. "Go on. He ain't gonna hurt you no more."

Reluctantly, the girl scampered to her feet.

"Put some clothes on, woman," Raider said, never taking his eyes off the clean-shaven outlaw.

Tipton started to get up.

Raider fired a shot in the wall above Tipton's head.

When the smoke cleared a little, Tipton glared at the bore of the Colt. "Are you loco?"

"No, just a honest workin' man in the service of Mr. Pinkerton. Now you move when I tell you or I'll blow your head off."

A faint smile came to Johnny's lips. "Pinkerton, huh? 'Smatter, can't the Fargo sheriff catch me?"

"Just hold still an' tell me where your guns are."

"Don't have no guns," Tipton said quickly. "Do I, honey? I don't have no guns. Can't carry guns in K.C. anymore."

The girl was gawking at Raider. "What'd he do? Why are you chasin' him?"

Raider sighed, almost hoping that Tipton would try something. "He robbed some, killed a few people."

"Others done worse," she offered.

"Yeah, I reckon," Raider replied. "But Johnny here did somethin' that nobody could forgive. Didn't you, boy?"

Tipton scowled back at him. "I don't know what the hell you're talkin' about, Pinkerton."

"Don't you, Johnny?"

The girl looked at Tipton. "What'd you do?"

"Shut up, bitch!"

Raider enjoyed watching the outlaw squirm. "See, honey, Johnny here had another girlfriend afore you."

"You bastard!" Tipton cried.

"Who?" the girl asked.

"Her name was Amanda," Raider continued. "Johnny roughed her up pretty good. Left her for dead. Only she weren't dead, Johnny. She lived. An' she can point t' you at the trial."

"No crime to treat a woman rough," the girl offered, defending her man to the end. "Some even like it."

"I never met one who liked to be hurt," Raider said. "It takes a sick kinda man t' hit a woman. Only Amanda weren't no woman."

The girl glared at Raider. "What do you mean?"

"Shut up!" Tipton cried.

Raider thumbed the hammer of the Colt, rattling the cylinder, pointing the bore at Tipton's head. "The next one's right b'tween your eyes, Johnny boy."

Tipton's face froze, his body was rigid.

"Tell me about Amanda," the girl insisted.

"She was only ten years old," Raider said. "An' Johnny hurt her bad. She'll live, but she'll see his hateful face for the rest o' her life. She'll never forgit what he did. She'll be afraid o' her own shadow, of every dark patch in the woods.

She'll always think another one like Johnny is out there."

"Shut the hell up, you Pinkerton bastard."

"You're comin' with me, Johnny. I'm gonna drag you down t' the police house t' lock you up. It's gonna be over for you real soon. You ever wondered what it'd be like t' die at the end of a rope? Your tongue hangs out, you swing 'round an' twitch. I bet Amanda's maw an' paw will be happy t' see that. Now, you're gonna do like I tell you. Understand?"

Raider was going to tell him to stand up slowly, to put his hands on top of his head.

Tipton started to lower his hands beneath the sheet.

"Do it and there won't be no hangin'," Raider told him.

"Just gettin' my pants."

"Up, slow, and then—"

The woman screamed. Raider turned to see her lunging at him with a knife. He managed to swing around, deflecting her attack with his gun hand. She missed with the blade, but Tipton got all the chance he needed. He lunged past Raider, flying down the hall.

Raider stepped out, firing a shot into the darkness. A door slammed. The woman leaped at him again, wielding the knife. Raider didn't like hitting a female, but this was a special case. He drew back and slammed a hard right on her chin. The girl fell backward, unable to attack him again.

Raider started down the hall.

Rosey came out of the shadows. "Where is he?"

"He ran," the big man replied. "That fine upstandin' citizen back there helped him escape. When she wakes up, tell her that she's under arrest."

"Really?"

"No, but tell her just t' put a scare on her."

He started toward the front door, thinking that it wouldn't be hard to find a naked man running through the streets of Kansas City.

Raider chased Tipton a long way. He had to give it to the outlaw; Johnny was resourceful. He managed to grab a man's duster as he fled, covering his naked body. Still, his trail was easy to follow, all the way to the cattle pens at the edge of town.

The damned pens were full.

Raider stepped up onto the rail of the corral, peering out over the heads of the steers. He could see Johnny Tipton moving through the herd. He was running low, parting the animals in his path.

Raider tried to take aim, but he didn't want to waste a shot. He only had three bullets left. Best to make them count.

Jumping down, he ran around the line of the corral, keeping his ear tuned to the complaints of the steers as Johnny disturbed their rest. Raider expected to beat Tipton to the other side and be waiting for him when he came out of the corral. The only problem was, Johnny Tipton was nowhere in sight when Raider got to the other end of the cattle pen.

"Damn."

Something rustled behind him.

Raider wheeled with the Colt but saw only shadows.

He looked back in the direction where Tipton had been running.

Nothing.

A dilapidated shed and some other structures stood ahead of him, about five or six hundred feet away. Had Tipton really gotten through the corral that fast? Maybe a scared man could have done it, made it all the way to those buildings.

Raider thought he heard footsteps. He listened, but the noise of the cattle seemed to well up, drowning out all other sounds. Something appeared to move over his shoulder. He looked back again into the shadows.

The cows kept bawling.

Raider peered toward the shed. Tipton had to be in there. Best to try it before he got away. He tried to start forward but it didn't happen. Something didn't feel right.

Jingling sounds, like spurs lifted in the night.

Behind him.

Raider eased toward the corral, watching, listening.

Spurs.

Man moving out of the shadows.

He had a shotgun or maybe a rifle.

Raider felt something on his back. He had run into the corral. Bouncing off, he faced the man who was coming toward him. Maybe the local constable had gotten word of the disturbance and had come to see for himself.

Stay still. Maybe he would pass by without seeing the big

man. Keep the Colt ready. The man couldn't be Tipton. Where would Tipton have gotten a shotgun? How did he—

The man turned toward him.

Raider nodded.

The man nodded back.

Raider started to speak but the man raised the bore of a twin-barreled scattergun.

Raider was going to shoot back until he heard the scream behind him.

He wheeled to see a shape against the sky, flying down on him like the darkest banshee from the bowels of the earth.

The shotgun exploded and a body fell dead to the ground.

Raider froze when he heard the scattergun go off.

The corpse of the flying man hit the earth with a dull thud.

Raider felt the sweat breaking on his face. He wheeled back to stare at the man with the shotgun, wondering if he was next. The man had fired both barrels so Raider could take him with the Colt. But something told him not to shoot.

He let out a deep breath. "Give me a reason not to kill you, mister."

No reply from the man, whose face was still hidden in darkness.

"I need a answer, mister, or I'll have ta—"

"Looked like that one was about to get you, Raider."

The big man grimaced, wondering where he had heard the voice before.

Coming closer, the shotgun man struck a match to light a ready-rolled cigarette. Raider saw the deep lines in the face, the reddish mustache. He still didn't have the name.

The man fanned out the match and tossed it to the ground. "I'd offer you one, Raider, but I know you don't smoke."

Who did he know who smoked ready-rolls?

"Reckon I saved your fatback, Raider. You owe me."

"How you figger?"

The man came closer still, kicking the corpse of Johnny Tipton. "He was about to dive right on you. Lookit there, has a piece of jagged metal in his hand. I reckon he wanted to cut your heart out."

"Most of 'em do."

He looked at the man, trying to come up with a name. "I give up, pardner."

"It's me, Raider. P. W. Avery."

Raider wanted to feel happy, but he knew better. "What the hell are you doin' here, P. W.? Hell, you walk in here an' throw me off."

"I saved your ass."

"You saved nothin', boy. I was on top o' this one till you came in here janglin' your spurs. Shit, if you hadn'ta confused me, I woulda caught this boy sooner or later."

P. W. Avery laughed cynically, like he had seen this act from Raider before. "Well, don't worry. I'll write the report for you and tell how it all happened. Want me to say you killed him?"

Raider sighed, turning away from his fellow Pinkerton agent to look at the body. "Say whatever you want. It don't matter now, at least not t' ol' Johnny." He nudged the corpse with his foot. "Good shot, though. You emptied both barrels. How'd you figger I wouldn't shoot you?"

Avery shrugged. "Just thought you was smarter than that." Avery laughed.

Raider shook his head, wondering how things had gotten so far out of hand. He glared at Avery. "How'd you find me anyway?"

"You ain't hard to find, Raider. Especially when the shooting started."

"The old man send you t' find me?"

"The old man is here," Avery replied in a puff of smoke.

Raider grimaced. "Pinkerton?"

"Wagner."

Raider looked down at the body. "Damn. He ain't gonna like this. We better get ol' Tipton here over t' the police house."

"I don't think Wagner is gonna care, Raider."

The big man wasn't sure he liked the sound of that. He wanted to ask Avery what he meant by the remark, but he was afraid he might not appreciate the answer. So he told Avery to pick up the dead man's feet. Wagner could wait until Johnny Tipton was resting in a pine box.

CHAPTER SEVEN

It took a while to square things with the local constabulary, but the remains of Johnny Tipton were finally laid to rest in back of the police house. Kansas City was big enough to have a couple of undertakers who would fight it out for the right to bury the lawbreaker. Raider figured that Tipton could stay in Missouri. No need to take him back to Fargo. He would have to recover any stolen goods from the whorehouse, maybe check at the stable to see if Tipton had a mount. Those wronged by Tipton were due some sort of compensation.

Perhaps the dread of meeting Wagner was enough to make Raider dawdle at the police house. P. W. Avery kept telling him to hurry, that it would be so nice to see the old man. Of course, Raider noticed that P. W. did not accompany him when the time came. When the big man called Avery on his cowardice, the surly agent replied that Wagner wanted to see Raider alone.

"What'd I do now?" Raider said as they walked toward the Royal House.

P. W. wiped sweat off his forehead. "I better leave you, Raider. I, er—well, there's another assignment I have to—"

"Aw, go on, Avery. I cain't blame you. I'd run away like a scared bird if I didn't haveta see him. What is it anyway?"

Avery shrugged. "I don't know. Somethin' big. Somethin' bad."

"What else?"

"So long, Raider."

"Get gone, P. W. An' hey—thanks for helpin' out."

"You never change, Raider. You never do."

"An' I don't plan to."

The big man turned and walked toward the entrance of the hotel.

When he entered the lobby of the Royal House, Raider tried to duck past the fish-eyed desk clerk. Wagner had to make it tough by staying at the same hotel as Raider. He wondered if his boss would still be up. Maybe he had stayed at the police house long enough so that everything would have to wait until morning.

The desk clerk squashed that notion. "Mr. Raider," he called as the big man walked by. "Could I see you a moment?"

Raider sighed and rolled his eyes. Nothing to do but listen to it. He slid over next to the desk.

"Mr. Wagner will receive you in room ten," the clerk offered. "He said you're to come immediately."

Raider nodded, adding out of guilt, "I'll pay my bill t'morrow. Didn't mean to let it—"

"Your bill has been taken care of," the clerk replied. "You'll be checking out tomorrow."

Raider grimaced. "Oh, I will, huh?"

"I suggest you see Mr. Wagner."

Raider suddenly felt riled. He didn't mind Wagner ordering him around from Chicago. It was one thing to get a telegram; it was another for the runty little office man to come into Raider's realm, pushing him around like he was a wet-eared schoolboy. Raider wanted to let Wagner know how he felt about the situation, so he started for the stairs.

"Room ten," the clerk called.

Raider didn't even knock. He opened the door and pushed into the chamber. Wagner stood next to the window, cleaning his wire-rimmed spectacles with a monogrammed handkerchief.

He donned the glasses and straightened his body. "It's

about time you got here," Wagner cried. "Why didn't you stay put like I told you?"

Raider thought the short-statured man looked like a tailor he had known in Denver, one of Doc Weatherbee's old buddies. "I didn't leave Kansas City," he replied. "An' I left the name o' this hotel at the telegraph office."

"And what have you been doing all this time?" Wagner challenged.

"Well, aside from waitin' for my back pay, I been lookin' for a boy name o' Johnny Tipton. He's the one from North Dakota who—"

"I told you to get off that case," Wagner said.

"Too late; I caught him. He's layin' over b'hind the police house, wrapped in a blanket an' covered with lye."

Wagner shook his head. "You killed him."

"Well, no, actually P. W. cut him in two with that shotgun o' his. Pretty as you please. There were guts strewed—"

"Spare me. And take off that hat!"

Raider removed his Stetson, watching as the man in the black suit began to pace back and forth. "Somethin', ain't it," Raider said, "bein' back here in Kansas City after all that mess you got into. Remember, Wagner, how me an' Doc pulled you outta the fire?"

"I see no reason to bring that up."

Raider gestured to the fancy chair in the corner of the room. "I've had a rough night, Wagner. Mind if I take a load off?"

Before his superior could reply, Raider eased into the chair, leaning back, stretching out his legs. "They said they'd bury Tipton here. I might be able t' find some o' the stuff he took. If I—"

Wagner waved him off. "I don't want to hear another word about Tipton," he replied. "That's not why I came."

Raider straightened a little in the chair. "I'm listenin', Wagner. It has t' be somethin' good t' bring you this far."

"Four of our agents are missing."

Raider squinted at his boss. "What the hell you mean by missin'?"

"In the last four months, I've sent four men to Idaho and not one of them has returned."

Raider shrugged. "You know how it is, boss. You get out

in the field an' you lose track o' time. Who'd you send anyway?"

"McGovern was first."

"Good man," Raider said. "Wouldn't wanna work with him though. Course, I don't wanna work with nobody."

Wagner glared at him. "Do you think you could resist babbling long enough to let me finish?"

"Doc usta say things like that t' me."

"Really?" Wagner smiled a little.

"It usta make me wanna kick his ass."

Wagner's smile vanished. "When McGovern didn't report back, I sent Walters to look for him."

Raider grimaced. "Big mistake there. Walters couldn't find his ass with four hands an' a San Francisco gaslight."

Wagner pointed a finger at the big man. "That kind of impertinence might get you fired someday."

"Sorry, Wagner." He tried hard not to grin. "Er, 'scuse me. Like I said, I had a rough night so far. An' I have a feelin' it ain't gonna get any easier. Who'd you send t' look for Walters?"

"Eagleton."

"And t' look for him?" Raider asked.

Wagner sighed deeply. "Stanton. I sent Stanton."

Raider sat up straight, perching on the end of the chair. Stanton was a good agent, better than Raider himself, or at least some said it. The big man from Arkansas had always felt a sense of competition with the rangy agent. Stanton usually got cases that were just as rough as the cases Wagner threw in Raider's direction.

"When'd he go in?" Raider asked.

"Over three weeks ago. I told him to check in with me every week, but I haven't heard from him since last month."

Raider rubbed his chin, thinking. "Well, the wires could be down. It's been awful rainy. Maybe he's been sendin' the messages but they ain't been gettin' through."

"Don't you think I've considered that?" Wagner replied impatiently. "I sent a wire to Boise to see if it would get through. The key operator's reply arrived less than an hour later."

"He's in trouble then," Raider asserted.

"Why do you say that?"

"Simple. Stanton does what you tell him. Don't he? He always goes by the book. That's the difference b'tween him an' me."

"You could stand to go a little more by the book, Raider."

Raider laughed. "Wagner, I wrote the damned book. And what I ain't already writ, I write it as I go along. You get me?"

"You could be relieved of your duties!" Wagner threatened.

"Any time, gopher-dick. Just give me my back pay an' I'll be outta here so fast you won't know what hit you!"

Wagner released a grunt of frustration. He knew he shouldn't let Raider's insubordination get to him. As much as he hated to admit it, the agency needed the big galoot's services. Raider would go anywhere, do anything, even if he went and did it with his own particular brand of roughhouse. The devil-may-care attitude still enraged Wagner and there didn't seem to be a thing the bespectacled gent could do about it.

So he decided to give Raider his back pay.

The big man just took the leather pouch full of money and put it in his shirt pocket.

Wagner glared at him. "Aren't you going to count it?"

Raider shrugged. "I'm sure it's what I got comin' t' me. You never make mistakes, do you Wagner?"

"I paid your hotel bill out of your wages."

"Forgit it. S'pose you tell me why you sent those four boys t' Idaho in the first place?"

"Have you ever heard of Robert Galler?"

Raider shook his head.

"He's owns a mining company in Idaho," Wagner went on. "Galler Mines, somewhere in the mountains."

"Silver?" Raider asked.

Wagner nodded. "Well-to-do as far as I can see. So far he's paid for every day that one of our agents has spent on the case."

"Four of our agents," Raider reminded him.

Wagner frowned. "This doesn't make us look good."

"I don't give a tinker's damn how it makes us look," Raider replied. "I wanna know what happened to them four. 'Cept for Walters, those other three was good agents."

"What have you got against Walters?"

The big man shrugged. "Nothin', really. He's just a desk

rider. Shouldn't be out in the field, at least not lookin' into dangerous notions."

Wagner could not really take umbrage with Raider's observation. He had sent Walters in the first place because he had been shorthanded. Raider was right. Walters was a desk rider. Too late to regret it now.

"S'pose you tell me why we're workin' for this Galler?" Raider asked.

"It seemed so simple at first," Wagner continued. "Galler's daughter Cynthia disappeared about seven weeks ago. Mr. Galler hired us to find her."

"Somebody nab her?"

"Galler suspects a man named Kreeger, Hunt Kreeger. It seems Kreeger was after Cynthia, wanting to marry her. Galler disapproved of Kreeger but Cynthia insisted on seeing him. Galler suspects Kreeger was meeting his daughter on the sly. Kreeger was the only one who could have taken Cynthia."

Raider studied on it for a spell, finally saying, "Mebbe the girl went with him on her own."

"Voluntarily?"

Raider nodded. "She was seein' him t' spite her daddy. Mebbe they up an'—?"

"Eloped."

"Yeah, 'loped. Funny name for it. But that could be what they did. It wouldn't be the first time it's happened."

Wagner agreed, but added, "That still doesn't explain the disappearance of our four men."

Raider exhaled. "No, it don't. So I reckon I better git goin'."

"Finally we agree on something," Wagner said. "Now, you'll be leaving on the train first thing in the morning."

"No, I'll be leavin' t'night on my horse."

Wagner glared at him again. "The train will be faster."

"Yep, but not if I take it out of Kansas City. I can catch it west o' here an' then find a steamer or maybe pick up another mount. If I go hard, I can be in Idaho by the end o' the month."

"The trail will be cold by then."

Raider stood up. "Not so cold I cain't foller it. You say this Galler lives in Boise?"

"He has an office there. I have the address."

"I'll find him. Boise ain't that big."

He started for the door.

Wagner called after him. "Raider, I want you to check in with me at least once a week."

Raider turned to glare at the little man. "That shit don't wash with me, Wagner."

"How dare you—"

"Every time I send a message from the telegraph office, word gets 'round there's a Pinkerton in the area. How much chance you think I got if I cain't disguise myself? Huh?"

Wagner seemed to deflate a little. "Well, I didn't stop to—I mean, I see your point—" Then, more forcefully, "But you had better—"

"Better what, Wagner? Huh?"

"You'd better find out what happened to our agents."

"I aim to, Wagner. I damned well aim to."

Wagner gestured toward the door. "Now get out of here and don't let me hear from you until you have results."

"Fine!" Raider hollered. "I'll do that!"

Wagner jumped when Raider slammed the door. The little man's stomach was churning. But somehow he felt a lot better. Raider was on the job. That was all Wagner could do. The case of the missing Pinkerton agents was now out of his hands.

Raider forgot about Wagner as soon as he left the hotel. He was ready to leave Kansas City anyway, even if it meant not getting to spend his back pay on whiskey, gambling, and women. Still, he had to clear up a few matters before he rode out. And all of them had something to do with Rosey.

She was bucking in the sack with a cowboy when Raider got there. The big man waited patiently for her to finish, thinking that he would have wanted to take another turn if he hadn't been forced to take sloppy seconds. Best just to finish the business with Rosey and go look for those missing men.

When the cowboy came out of her room, he gaped at Raider in alarm.

"Don't worry," the big man said. "I ain't the law. But you better clear out in a hurry."

The cowboy didn't have to be told twice.

Rosey smiled at him when Raider eased into the room.

"Honey, you brought me luck. I've been busier tonight than a cat with two assholes."

Raider's eyes narrowed. "Where is it, Rosey?"

She stiffened. "What are you talkin' about?"

"Johnny Tipton had money on him. He had his stuff here. Prob'ly his saddlebags. I'm bettin' you picked it all up after I cold-cocked that girl."

Rosey sighed defeatedly. "Never could sneak anything past you, Raider."

She reached under the bed and pulled out the saddlebags that used to belong to Johnny Tipton.

"How much was in there?" Raider asked.

Rosey glared at him. "What makes you think I counted it?"

"How much?"

She exhaled again. "Four hundred."

"It's gotta go back t' the people he took it from," Raider offered. "I wouldn't care if you kept every penny, but—"

"There goes my house in Liberty." Her voice cracked a little.

Raider remembered the money in his shirt pocket. "How much you need?"

She gazed up hopefully. "The house is two hundred and fifty dollars."

"So how much you need?"

"Another hundred oughta do it. Maybe another fifty for the kitty, just to make sure I can live for a while until I build up my old trade again."

Raider reached into his pocket and threw her the pouch. "Count it."

"Where'd you get this?" she asked, opening the purse.

"Back pay."

She counted for a minute or so. "You must be doin' pretty good," she said. "There's a hundred and eighty dollars here."

"I just ain't been paid for a long time," Raider replied. "Look, you take a hundred an' thirty an' leave me fifty. I'm goin' on another case, so I'll need some money."

She counted it out, never hesitating. "Thank you, Raider. You got a lifetime of free humps comin', whenever you're in Liberty." She put his fifty back in the pouch and returned it to him.

It sort of made him feel good to give her the money. "Now,

Rosey, you promise you'll go buy that house t'morrow. Don't stay 'round this bad part o' town any longer 'n you haveta."

"I'm hopin' you're gonna stay around, Raider. After all, you did give me this money and I figure you ought to have somethin' comin' to you."

He thought about following a night's worth of cowboys. "Thanks anyway, Rosey, but I—"

Her hand slid up his leg to his crotch. "I can suck it, honey."

Before he could protest, she went to work on his buttons.

She did the same trick with her false teeth, only this time Raider didn't release.

"Lay back," he said, wondering if he would regret it.

She spread out on the bed, opening her thighs. "As deep as you can get it, cowboy."

He entered her and immediately knew that it wasn't going to be bad at all.

Wagner looked up when Raider entered his room.

The big man tossed the saddlebags on the floor at Wagner's feet. "This is the stuff Johnny Tipton stole. I'm trustin' you t' send it back t' Fargo."

"Just couldn't resist finishing the case," Wagner said with a wry smile.

"Don't wanna ruin my reputation, William."

"Get the hell out of here."

"Goin' t' Idaho, William. Goin' t' Idaho."

He slammed the door again.

Wagner picked up the saddlebags, thinking the big man from Arkansas had no peer, there was no one else like him.

Thank God, Wagner thought. *Thank God.*

CHAPTER EIGHT

Raider hadn't told Wagner the exact truth when he said he could get west faster by leaving Kansas City that night. Of course, he wouldn't have to wait around for the train the next morning, which would give him a head start. But the train might have been a little quicker, providing no unfortunate accidents befell the locomotive. Trains could derail, break down, reach bridges that had fallen into a river and have to stop.

With his justifications fresh in his mind, Raider rode the roan out of Kansas City, never looking back after he crossed the Missouri. He had a plan in mind: ride to Salina, where he could sell his mount for a good price to a fair horse trader. In Salina, he could pick up a train to Utah, which would put him on the southern border of Idaho. There he could buy another horse and ride north to Boise. As much as he hated riding the train, it was the best way to get to Idaho.

The big man was anxious to get on the trail. He didn't like the idea of his own colleagues disappearing. Even if they might really be safe and sound, hot on a case, unable to get to a wire to send a message to Wagner. Wagner worried too much, Raider thought. Best not to get your spurs in a tangle, at least until you knew what you were up against.

On the ride to Salina, he considered the possibilities in the case of the missing girl. Her disappearance might not be as serious as everyone thought. Surely not as serious as the missing Pinkerton agents.

The first thought that crossed his mind was that the girl and her beau had simply eloped, leaving for parts unknown. Maybe the young man had some sort of grubstake. The loving couple might have bought a farm or a store, they might be living happily in some small town. He could be a blacksmith, she could take in wash and sewing until the first baby came.

He decided to take things further, in a darker direction.

What if the beau was a hound, the kind who was after the money of the girl's father? Maybe the girl had been the one to suggest they elope. The beau had been forced into it, to prove his love. Maybe he'd dump her somewhere down the trail, leaving her along the way. In such a case, she'd probably come dragging home to daddy; that is, if she survived the trip home.

Take it deeper, into the pit.

What if the beau was the kind to kill her when he was finished with her? Somewhere along the ride he would realize that he was not going to get any of her daddy's money. Here he was, stuck with her, wishing he had never brought her along. What else could he do but put a bullet in her one night? He'd have to choose the right place, where nobody would hear the shot. Bury her in a small grave and move on.

Raider decided to come back a little.

Now it seemed to him that if the beau was looking for money from the girl's father, at some point he would have asked for it. Maybe try to get the old man to come across with a big payoff, demanding a sizeable sum to get out of his daughter's life. When this didn't work, the beau talks the girl into running off with him so that he can demand ransom later. That would make sense as much as anything.

Of course, it was all speculation until Raider got to Boise, to personally demand the details and facts from Mr. Galler himself.

He had trouble thinking about the girl when he considered that four of his own kind might be in trouble somewhere in the mountains of Idaho. Maybe there was something that had cornered them, something that had nothing—or everything—to do with the disappearance of the girl. He spurred the roan, making for Salina with a newfound sense of devotion to the case.

In Salina, the horse trader gave him a fair price for the roan. Raider tucked the money away, saving it for the mount he would have to purchase in Utah.

He dragged his saddle and the rest of his gear over to the porch of the general store, where he waited with a few other cowboys for the train. They were honest hands who were heading west to work in California and Montana. Raider bought a wedge of cheese, some bread, and a bottle of corn liquor, all of which he shared with the cowboys. The train showed up a few hours later to take them away.

When Raider boarded, he informed the conductor that he was a Pinkerton agent. The conductor immediately asked him to ride for free, in the mail car. They could use the extra protection. Rumor had it that a band of train robbers was operating along the line.

Raider patted his Winchester and told the conductor that there was nothing to be afraid of.

The train pulled out of Salina right on time.

Raider settled back on his saddle, snoozing in the mail car. Nothing to worry about. Not as long as he had his rifle.

And there wasn't a bit of trouble, until they crossed over the border into Utah.

The whole trip had been pretty easy. Raider had slept most of the way, dreaming of women he had known. The mail clerk, a man named Jody, was a quiet sort who kept a small bottle of "cough medicine" hidden in his desk. He kept his mouth shut and shared a few drinks with Raider, which made him a perfect traveling companion.

So the big man caught up on his rest, waking at a station stop now and then to eat and drink and take care of other necessities. Then it was back to the mail car, using his saddle for a pillow. He was dreaming about a cathouse in Mexico when the train screeched to a stop.

Raider slid across the floor of the mail car when the engineer hit the brakes. He sat up quickly, looking around him, trying to get his bearings. He couldn't remember where the hell he was. In the cathouse? No, he had been dreaming about that. He was on a train, somewhere between Colorado and Utah. And he was on his way to Idaho.

Jody, the mail clerk, was standing on his desk, gazing out of the slit that served as a window for the mail car.

Raider started to crawl back toward his saddle.

"It's a holdup," Jody said.

Raider reached for his gun belt, which was wrapped around the saddle horn. "You sure 'bout that?"

Jody nodded, climbing down. "Yeah. There's five or six of them. Probably got tree trunks blocking the tracks. That's why the engineer had to lay down so hard on the brake."

Raider stood up, strapping his gun belt around his waist. He checked the empty cylinder of the Colt and slid in the sixth cartridge. Then he reached down for his Winchester.

Jody looked at both weapons in his hands. "There's too many of them, Raider. You'll never—"

"Shh, I gotta listen. What the hell time is it anyway?"

"After midnight."

Raider nodded. "Makes sense. Ever'body's sleepy. Stop the train an' take ever'thin'."

He slid closer to the door, trying to decipher the noises he heard outside. Horses, more than three, less than eight. Voices from men on horseback. Tack jangling, mounts snorting.

"I told you there were—"

Raider waved off the clerk. "Shh."

Outside, a deep voice called orders. "Get their money. Hurry it up. Get the rings from the women and the watches from the men."

Raider looked at the mail clerk, who had turned as white as a sheet. "Jody, I think these boys has done this afore."

"The Sand gang," the clerk replied. "They hit us two months ago. As soon as you think they're gone, they're back again."

"He's got 'bout six or seven of 'em out there. I'm bettin' one is holdin' a gun on the engineer."

The mail clerk frowned. "Listen."

Raider could hear the men outside the car.

Jody backed away from the noise. "They're comin' for the strongbox."

Raider stepped back a few feet, holstering the Colt.

Somebody knocked hard on the door of the boxcar. "Okay, boy, open up."

Jody just stood there.

Another knock, probably with the butt of a pistol. "I said open up. If we have to take a ax to this thing, I'm gonna chop you up an' bury you in the strongbox."

Raider took a deep breath. He was angry more than scared. This outlaw had disturbed his sleep. It was always a mistake to awaken a sleeping animal. The first thing it did was turn on you.

One more decisive knock. "Open this damned door, boy. I mean it."

Raider rattled the lever of his Winchester.

"What should I do?" asked the trembling clerk.

Raider slipped an extra cartridge into the side of the rifle. "Open the door for him, Jody. Just like he said. Open the damned door."

The clerk wasn't sure he liked the glassy look in Raider's black eyes, but he obeyed the big Pinkerton and slid open the boxcar door.

The train robbers weren't expecting rifle shots from the boxcar. They had their weapons lowered, waiting for the clerk as if they did not fear him. Instead of the strongbox, the gang got rapid rifle fire. Raider let out a rebel yell, firing the Winchester as fast as he could pump the lever. Three men fell immediately, trampled by the hooves of their own frenzied mounts.

Shots resounded from the passenger section of the train. Raider eased back into the boxcar, listening. Four left, maybe five. Man on the engine. Maybe six of them. He reloaded the rifle.

Jody was gaping wide-eyed as the smoke drifted in the air. "That was great shootin', mister."

"Stick around," Raider replied. "I'm goin' up top. Is there any way t' git 'tween the cars without showin' myself?"

Jody pointed to the ceiling. "There's a small trapdoor on the ceiling. Use it for air sometimes, but you might be able to get through it."

The opening was a tight fit, but Raider managed to squeeze onto the roof of the boxcar. Jody passed his rifle to him. As

Raider started to stand up, another Winchester exploded, sending a slug over his head.

Raider wheeled toward the caboose, firing three times in the direction of the muzzle flash. A man cried out and fell to the ground. Raider stayed low, wondering if any of the others had come aloft. He had killed four. Maybe there were eight of them.

He started along the top of the train, using his rifle for balance as he leaped between the cars.

Something rustled to his left, below him. One rider started away, fleeing on his horse. Raider cut him down with three shots. Two more pistols fired up at him. He hit the deck and crawled a few feet.

How many of them were there?

Another man ran out to look up into the night shadows. Raider hit him between the eyes with one shot. Two more men broke for freedom. Raider dispatched them to perdition, but he had to empty the damned rifle to do it.

When the running men fell, Raider just lay there, listening again. He could hear the cries of passengers below. Luckily he had managed to strike before the gang got the passengers out of the day car. How many men were inside, waiting to fire on him?

Raider crawled to the front end of the car, looking for a way down. He had to feel his way in the dark. Get inside, try to shoot straight so he wouldn't hit any innocent bystanders.

Suddenly two voices came out of the train. "Where is he?"

"I don't know."

"There must be more than one."

"I'd say about six of them."

"Probably Pinkertons or marshals."

Raider grinned. "Come on out, boys. You're surrounded. The mail car was full o' hired guns. Come out with your hands up an' we won't shoot you."

After a few minutes, both gunmen came out reaching for the sky.

Raider called down to the passengers. "Get 'em an' tie 'em up."

Eager for revenge, the train riders swarmed on the robbers, beating them to the ground. Raider stood up, looking toward the engine. There had to be a man on the engineer. It just plain made sense.

He started along the roof, jumping between cars until he arrived at the coal car. Only the train wasn't burning coal. The car had been stacked with hardwood. Raider crouched low, peering toward the engine.

He couldn't see much but finally the voices became clear.

"What's goin' on back there?"

A weaker voice, probably the engineer. "Please, don't hurt anybody."

Raider eased down into the fuel car, balancing on the stacks of wood. Slowly he made his way toward the engine, inching silently forward. In a few minutes he peeked over the edge of the car, into the engineer's cab. A gunman held the barrel of a Colt to the engineer's neck. He kept looking around the edge of the cab, watching for his compatriots.

Lifting a chunk of hardwood, Raider tossed it over the side of the car. When it thudded to the ground, the gunman let go of the engineer. He came toward Raider, into full view. The big man from Arkansas lifted another piece of wood and threw it at the gunman's head.

The outlaw buckled, falling off the engine, rolling off the track bed into the dirt. Raider climbed down to make sure the man was out. But the man wasn't out. He was dead.

"Shoulda grabbed a smaller piece o' wood," Raider muttered.

When he climbed back into the cab, the engineer raised his hands. "Just don't hurt anyone, mister."

"I ain't gonna hurt no one," Raider said impatiently. "And if you wanna know the truth, I done stopped these boys from robbin' your train."

"Bless you," the engineer said.

"Well, I don't know 'bout that, but I better get ever'body t'gether so we can move those logs off the track."

"I'll help, sir. Hey, you're the Pinkerton."

"Yeah, I am. I killed most of 'em. I got two prisoners back there. Your passengers made short work of 'em."

"What should we do with the prisoners?" the engineer asked.

"I don't care," Raider replied. "An' I ain't writin' no report, I ain't buryin' no bodies, an' I sure as hell ain't gonna lose no more sleep. We're gonna clean up this mess an' then you're gonna get me the hell t' Utah so I can buy me a horse. Understood?"

The engineer said he understood perfectly.

CHAPTER NINE

Raider rode into Boise on a gray gelding that he had purchased in Blue Creek, Utah. The sturdy animal had carried him north, into the heart of the Idaho territory. Gold had once ruled the region, and it was still around, silver was the new king and it sometimes ruled with a violent hand. Raider had seen more than one man who had killed for the gray metal they turned into dimes and two-bit pieces and silver dollars. Like gold, silver had its own demons. Raider couldn't really stand either one of them.

As the gray plodded steadily up the main, dirty street, Raider kept his head bent low, hiding under the brim of his Stetson. It was a dark, rainy day, the kind where everybody kept his head down. Good for not getting recognized, even when you were a stranger riding into a new town.

Nobody gave him a second look as he tied the gray in front of the Galler Mining offices. He hesitated for a moment, peering into the bright enclosure that was lighted with gas lamps. Business as usual. He wondered how worried Galler was about his daughter.

When he pushed through the front door, he saw that the outer office was empty. A bell tinkled as he closed the door behind him. Immediately, a well-groomed man appeared from the back rooms.

"Yes?"

Raider eyed him, thinking he was too young to be Galler. Slicked-back, black hair, thin mustache, black suit. A weak face, but clear brown eyes that peered straight at the big man.

"I'm lookin' for Mr. Galler."

The dapper man smiled. "Perhaps I can help you. I'm Harold Burden. I work for Mr. Galler."

"Kinda wanted t' see Mr. Galler," Raider offered. "Wanted t' talk t' him in person."

"Do you have an appointment with him?"

"Well, no."

"Do you know him? Or does he know you? Perhaps if you gave me your name, I could pass a message along to him."

"Well, I'd—"

"Harry, what's the trouble?"

An older gentleman stuck his head into the room. He was tall, well-groomed, with thick salted red hair. Pale skin, droopy cheeks, sad blue eyes. He glanced quizzically at Raider.

"Who is this man?"

Burden smiled at his boss. "He wants to see you, Mr. Galler. He says he has to talk to you in person."

Galler frowned at Raider. "I have no business with this man."

Raider grinned. "Well, sir, your name is on the door an' I like t' speak t' the head man when I ask for a job."

"What kind of job?" Galler asked.

"Anythin', sir. I've mined afore, I've rode shotgun on a payroll wagon. Anythin' you need."

Galler waved him off. "I'm not hiring."

"I can do—"

Burden interceded. "He's not hiring, sir. I suggest you try the Union City Silver Company. Perhaps they can use your services."

Raider started to say something else, but Galler had already gone back into the other room. So the big man just tipped his hat and excused himself. As he walked across the street toward the saloon, he could hear Wagner's voice in his head. Wagner was asking why Raider had come all this way just to lie to Galler. But the big man had a plan. And he aimed to follow through with it. He didn't want to end up missing, like his associates. It wasn't part of his plan.

For the rest of the gloomy day, Raider watched the offices of Galler Mining. He waited until Robert Galler emerged and started along the wooden sidewalk. The tall gentleman picked his way between the mud puddles, no doubt heading for home. When he had gone far enough, Raider fell in behind him and followed Galler to a white house on the edge of town.

Galler entered the neatly painted house, lighting one lamp when he was inside. Raider sat behind a tree across the street, waiting until darkness replaced the gray shadows of the day. Then he headed for the rear of the white house, looking for a back entrance.

The back door wasn't locked. Maybe Galler was leaving it open, hoping that his girl would come home. Maybe he was just careless in his grief.

Raider stepped slowly through the shadows, making for the one lighted room. Galler sat alone in what appeared to be his den. He was slouched in a chair, his face in his hands. His head snapped up as Raider eased into the room. He looked scared.

"What the devil are you doing here?" Galler cried, his voice cracking.

Raider held up his hand. "Easy there, captain. I have a feelin' you're gonna be glad t' see me when you find out who I really am."

"I told you, there's no work in my mines. I can't do anything for you. Do you hear me?"

"I'm not a miner," Raider replied. "I'm a Pinkerton agent. The fifth Pinkerton agent you've seen. And I wanna find out what happened t' the other four. Comprende?"

Galler glared at him. "If you're a Pinkerton, why didn't you present yourself as such when you came to my office today?"

Raider shrugged. "I wanted t' git a look at you, so I'd know who you were. That way I could follow you home an' see you in secret. I'm bettin' that the other four agents made themselves known t' you right away. An' I'm also bettin' that they've suffered for it."

Galler's face slacked a little. "Four men. And none of them came back with any news of my Cynthia."

"Mebbe I can change all that, Galler. But you haveta go along with me. You cain't tell nobody who I am."

Galler eyed him suspiciously. "How do I know who you really are? You say you're a Pinkerton, but I haven't seen any proof. And look at you. You're dressed more like a saddle tramp than a detective. The other men who called here wore suits. And they didn't have their guns slung low on their hips like gunfighters."

Raider reached into his shirt pocket, taking out his Pinkerton credentials. "I may not look like the others, but there's a reason for that. Go on, take a gander. I know you've seen papers like 'em afore. Four times t' be exact."

Galler studied the credentials and then began to cry.

Raider wasn't ready for the sudden flow of tears. The man seemed to crumble right before him. Raider asked for whiskey. Galler pointed to a cabinet on the wall.

"We both need a snort," Raider said.

Galler put his face in his hands. "She was the only thing I had. Cindy was everything to me. Now I have nothing. He took her, that Kreeger. I'll never see her again."

Raider had the liquor bottle in hand, pouring fine whiskey into two glasses. "You'll see her agin," he said. "I promise."

If she's still alive, the big man thought.

After a few drinks, Galler began to talk. The tale sounded as if he had rehearsed it, although Raider allowed for the fact that Galler had repeated it four times before. The basic story was the same one Wagner told, only this time the details were sketched in.

Hunt Kreeger had come to work for Mr. Galler as a surveyor. They had been working together to stake out some new mining sites north of Galler's current digs. Galler's company was in trouble. There hadn't been a new strike in over a year and the old mines were almost depleted. Galler had spent a lot of money searching for new strikes, not to mention the expenses of keeping the mines open. In short, he was close to being broke. His daughter's abduction had been the final insult from fate.

"Kreeger stole her heart," Galler said. "I knew she would

leave me someday. But you see, before her mother died, I promised that I would make sure Cindy married a fine young man, someone we could be proud of."

Raider nodded, thinking. "This Kreeger, was he handsome?"

"I suppose. Cindy took to him immediately. I know I kept her sheltered. And he seemed to be a man of the world."

"Was he a good surveyor?" Raider asked.

Galler frowned. "That's a funny question. I don't know. I never saw any of his finished work. Harry always took care of that."

"Burden?"

"Yes. We finally decided not to dig in the north. It didn't pan out. Harry showed me some figures. Just more bad news."

Raider shifted in the chair, a little numb from the good whiskey. "How long has Burden been with you?"

"I don't think that's any of your business!"

"You want your daughter back?"

Galler huffed a little, no longer sad but angry. "None of the others asked personal questions."

"I told you afore, I ain't the others. You gotta go along with me, Mr. Galler. I need t' see this thing from all corners of the barnyard. What seems nothin' t' you, might be the whole shootin' match t' me."

"I can't question Harry's loyalty! And you shouldn't either."

"I just asked how long has he been with you."

Galler sighed. "Almost two years. And he hasn't let me down once. Why, I don't know what I'd do without Harry. He's been a friend to me through all of this. More than a friend. He's like a son to me."

"Okay, okay. I was just askin'. Let's get back to Kreeger. Have you heard from him since he ran off with the girl?"

"Not a word."

Raider rubbed his stubbled face, ruminating. "Damn. There goes one o' my notions down the river."

"What are you talking about?"

"Well, Mr. Galler, my first thought on all this was that Kreeger was after your money. But did he know you're not doin' so well?"

Galler shrugged. "I don't think so. I never talked to him about it. I hated him too much to discuss my finances with him."

"Your daughter could've told him."

Galler blushed. "I'll thank you not to drag her through the mire."

"Beggin' your pardon, sir, but she's the one who started all this. She's gone an' four Pinks went with her. I'm bettin' the only way I can find my men is t' find your daughter. Or at least I might pick up somethin' along the trail t' give me a clue."

"I'm sorry," Galler said, "I want to help you. But I don't know where Kreeger took her. And I haven't heard from him since she disappeared."

"Mebbe he knows you're broke," Raider replied. "Holdin' her till you get into the chips."

"You think he wants ransom?"

"Mebbe. But he ain't gonna ask for it if he knows you ain't got it."

Galler shook his head from side to side, emitting a low moan. "Damn him. Damn him. I know he took her. I know it."

Raider poured him another shot of whiskey. "Drink up, Galler. It might help you sleep."

The tired man threw back the shot.

"Who took her ain't the problem," Raider said. "Where he took her an' why is the important thing. You don't have any thoughts as t' where he mighta took her?"

"If I knew, I'd be combing the area myself. I'd have already found her. Besides, I hired your men to find her. And what good did it do me?"

"Didn't do my men much good either," Raider offered.

"I'm sorry. I'm truly sorry. My God, I don't know your name."

"They call me Raider."

"Raider. An odd name."

"Yeah, I reckon."

They sat silently for a while, drinking.

Finally Raider stood up.

"Where are you going?" Galler asked.

"Well, first I'm gonna stable my horse. Then I'm gonna find a place t' sleep."

"You can stay here. You're welcome to my hospitality."

"I appreciate it, Mr. Galler, but I don't want nobody t' know I'm a Pinkerton agent workin' for you. You might haveta hire me a little later on, in case I need a excuse t' go north t' your mines."

"Why would you want to do that?"

Raider tipped back his Stetson. "Don't ask me t' explain my ways, sir. I work the way I please and that's that. I ain't got the best brain inside my noggin, but I use what's there. I follow a thing till it seems right. And I ain't never missed yet."

"You really think you can find my daughter?"

Raider braced for it, wondering how it would sound out loud. "If she's still alive."

Galler's eyes narrowed, his face contorted into an expression of rage. "How dare you say something like that!"

"Because you hadta hear it, Galler. Because it might be true. Kreeger might've backed into something he couldn't get outta. A woman has a way of makin' a man do funny things."

"She wasn't a woman—isn't a woman. She's a girl!"

"I don't wanna speak mean of her, sir, but it takes two horses t' make a team."

"Shut up! Shut up!"

"I'm sorry, Mr. Galler, but it hadta be said."

"Just go. If you want to talk to me again, come back tomorrow."

Raider hesitated by the door to the den. "Am I still on the case?"

Galler nodded.

"I wanna hear you say it."

"All right, you're still on the case. Find my daughter."

Raider nodded respectfully. "Just one more thing. I need t' know how t' find Harold Burden."

Galler bristled, but then gave him directions.

Raider started out, making for the back door, wondering if the night held any surprises.

CHAPTER TEN

As Raider walked down the dark street, there was no doubt in his mind that Robert Galler was sincere in his grief. He wore the sleepless look of a man beset by too many problems. His business was failing, his daughter was gone. Galler's whole life seemed to be unraveling like the thread from a cheap horse blanket.

At least he had been cooperative, although he probably had little faith in the abilities of the Pinkerton agents who had come before Raider. All four men had failed to find Cynthia Galler and had disappeared along with her in the bargain. Raider just hoped he could root out some sort of trail to lead him in the right direction. He wasn't the kind to poke around in the dark, not for long anyway. He needed facts, not many of them, but enough.

One useful bit of information had come up. Galler had pegged Hunt Kreeger as a surveyor. Surveyors had to be registered, they had to be legal. They went to school and logged documents in government offices. If Hunt Kreeger was really a surveyor, he was on record somewhere. Raider wondered if his predecessors had taken such a route in their investigations.

The big man stopped, assessing his location. He had followed the directions given him by Galler. Harold Burden lived in a small room overlooking a dark alley near the livery. Raider stopped on the corner, gazing up at the apartment. No lights were on. He decided to get his mount and stable it before he went to see Burden.

When he returned with the gray gelding behind him, Raider saw that Burden's light was on. He banged on the livery door until the farrier came to take the gelding. Raider paid him for two days in advance, in case he had to ride out in a hurry. He considered asking the livery man about Burden and Kreeger, but he decided to wait. Questions brought gossip and gossip led to speculation. Raider wanted to operate in secret as long as possible.

He was even reluctant to reveal himself to Burden, but he knew it was necessary. Raider had experience with weasels and he had tricks for rooting them out. How many times had he seen a man's own kin do him wrong? How many times was a man betrayed by his closest associates?

As he came out of the stable, he looked up at Burden's window. A light glowed there now. Best to let him get settled in. Raider began to consider what kind of questions he wanted to ask. If Burden cooperated, then he was probably in the clear. If he hindered the investigation, Raider would have to keep a closer watch on him.

Raider glanced up at the light again. Shadows were moving on the walls of Burden's place. He wasn't alone. Raider started for the stairs that led up to the apartment. He wanted to get a look at Burden's company.

As his foot hit the first step, the shouting began. Raider stopped, listening. He couldn't make out the words but the tone was clearly that of an argument. Then a gun went off and Raider was running up the stairs, laying his shoulder into the front door.

The lock splintered the jamb.

Raider shoved his way into the room. The body of Harold Burden was lying on the floor. He had been shot through the head with a small caliber weapon. Raider realized that he had drawn his own Colt.

A breeze stirred the curtains of a back window.

Raider heard footsteps on the roof outside the casement.

Raider stepped over the body, peering out into the darkness. Someone was scuffling toward the edge of the roof. Raider fired but the man slipped over the eaves, dropping to the ground.

The big man was going to follow until he heard the hooves of the horse galloping away.

He turned back to look at the body of Harold Burden.

"Damn."

Burden had turned from suspect to victim in a hurry. So much for that. Raider had to get his mount, to follow the killer. What the hell was going on anyway? He bent for a moment, to see if Burden might still be alive.

"Son of a bitch."

Holstering his weapon, Raider made for the stairs again. He hurried down the alley, back to the livery. He was banging on the door when he felt the hard nudge of a gun bore in his back.

"Stay real still," a deep voice said.

Raider hesitated, wondering if he should try it.

"You're under arrest, mister," the man said. "Now raise those hands against the door."

"Jimmy? Jimmy King?" Raider asked.

"King ain't the sheriff no more," the man replied. "I am."

"I knowed Jimmy," Raider offered. "I used to work with him. My name is Raider. I'm a Pinkerton agent."

"Maybe you are and maybe you ain't," the new sheriff replied.

Raider tried to look over his shoulder. "Let me turn around, Sheriff. Let me look at you. I'll keep my hands up."

The new sheriff reached for Raider's Colt, lifting it from the holster. When the gun was in his hand, the man backed away. "All right, turn around. But keep those hands to the sky."

Raider turned to stare down at a short, stocky man. The sheriff had a shiny Winchester pointed at his chest. One burst at this range would kill Raider no matter how fast he moved.

The sheriff lifted the bore of the Colt to his nose. "You just fired this gun. I was on my rounds. I heard it."

Raider nodded. "That's right, pardner. What d' they call you?"

"Jenkins, Tom Jenkins."

"What happened t' King?"

"Got hisself killed," Jenkins replied. "He was lookin' for that Galler girl. Never came back."

"That's it!" Raider insisted. "I'm here lookin' for four Pinks who never came back neither."

Jenkins held up the Colt. "Then how come you were shootin'?"

"I can show you," the big man said. "Up at Burden's. You know him?"

"Can't say as I do. I know who he is. Works over there for Mr. Galler."

"Not anymore," Raider replied.

"What you mean by that?" the sheriff asked.

"Come on, if you'll let me show you."

Jenkins was reluctant, but he finally followed Raider up the stairs.

The sheriff grimaced when he saw the body of Harold Burden. Blood had dried on the dead man's forehead. The bullet hole was no bigger than the head of a pocket revolver cartridge.

"Shot him with a small gun," Raider offered. "Close range. Then the killer went out the window and rode off on a horse. Had the mount waitin' for him."

Raider started toward the body. "Look here—"

The sheriff stopped him with the rifle. "Don't move, boy."

Raider's eyes narrowed. "Look here, Jenkins, you don't think I did this, d' you?"

Jenkins kept his eyes on Raider's hands. "I thought I told you to reach for the ceiling."

Raider hesitated, but then raised his palms. "Jenkins, you're keepin' me from catchin' the one who did this. If I can get on his trail, I might be able t' find him afore mornin'."

Jenkins looked at the body again and then back at Raider. "I catch you at the livery tryin' to get to your horse. Your gun is still hot."

"I told you, I fired at the one who was runnin' away. He went out the window and dropped to his horse."

"He? You know who it was?"

"I'm just guessin'," the big man replied. "It was prob'ly a man."

"How I know you wasn't in cahoots with him?"

Raider exhaled. "I got my Pinkerton papers in my pocket.

Or you can go ask Robert Galler who I am. I tell you, I came here to look for his missin' daughter. Ain't that enough for you?"

The sheriff asked to see his Pinkerton papers. Raider moved slowly, reaching into his shirt pocket. Jenkins looked them over but then shook his head.

"I'm sorry, boy, but I gotta hold you."

Raider grimaced. "You're makin' a big mistake, Sheriff."

"Maybe so, but you're all I got. And I aim to keep you until this is cleared up. Now, you comin' peaceable? Or do I have to shoot you?"

Raider said he would come peaceably, but he added that the sheriff should go ask Robert Galler to confirm Raider's identity.

Jenkins said he would, as soon as Raider was behind bars.

Raider sat in lockup for a while, expecting the sheriff to come right back from Galler's place to let him loose.

He was expectant when Jenkins returned to the jailhouse.

"Did Galler tell you who I was?" Raider asked.

The sheriff frowned. "Partner, Mr. Galler was nowhere to be found. He wasn't at his home or his office."

Raider felt a sinking feeling in his gut. "What?"

"'Fraid I'm gonna have to hold you until I find out who you really are," Jenkins said. "I know you got them papers, but those things can be bogus. And as far as I can see, you're gonna be held for the murder of Harold Burden. Of course, you'll get a trial as soon as the circuit judge gets back. You'll get a chance to say your piece."

Raider felt a tightening in his neck. "Damn, you're gonna hang me for somethin' I didn't do."

"Better go get that body."

"Sheriff, wait a minute. Look at my Colt and then look at the hole in Burden's head. If I had plugged him at that range, his innards would be splattered all over the room. He was shot with a small caliber gun. And go back underneath his window. You'll see a horse was there. Go on, you'll see."

The sheriff sighed, almost like he believed the big man. "If you're innocent, boy, I should be able to prove it."

"Wire my agency in Chicago," Raider offered as a last resort. "William Wagner will speak for what I've told you. I didn't kill that man."

"I hope not. I'd hate to hang an innocent man."

Raider put his face against the bars of the cell. "Sheriff, Galler's prob'ly in trouble too. I left him not one hour before Harold Burden was killed. Somebody might've took him, probably the same one what took his daughter."

"I'll see to it," the sheriff replied.

Raider watched him go. He had to admit that things didn't look too good for him. He didn't see Jenkins for the rest of the night. He couldn't sleep in the ratty cell, so he just sat there until morning, trying to think things out. He had to get on the trail, especially if Galler had been abducted. Maybe the mining man wasn't kidnapped at all. Maybe he was behind some of the strange happenings around Boise.

Just after daybreak the hammering started. Raider raised himself to look out the barred window. He could see the edge of the structure as it went up. He was pretty sure they were building a gallows. And he had to think that the hanging was going to be his own.

CHAPTER ELEVEN

Around noon that same day, Sheriff Jenkins returned to the jailhouse with a tray of food.

"My last meal?" Raider asked.

Jenkins just unlocked the cell door and invited Raider to sit at his own desk. "Food ain't bad," he said. "Fried steak and potatoes. A few string beans too."

Raider dug in, unsure of his status with the lawman. "I thought you said I'd have a trial."

"Nope," Jenkins replied. "Won't be necessary."

"Just gonna go ahead and hang me, huh?"

Jenkins grimaced, like he felt pain. "I did like you said, Raider. I went back to look at the body. You were right. Your gun couldn't have made that small wound. More than likely it was a pocket pistol, or some kind of derringer."

"What'd I tell you?"

"I also went back behind the building where Burden stayed," the sheriff continued. "Found horse tracks just like you said. Also found this."

He held up a small cartridge for Raider to see.

"Where'd you find it?" the big man asked.

"In one of the horse tracks. Looks like the killer loaded up in the dark, before he climbed up to Burden's place. Probably waitin' for Burden when he got home."

Raider shook his head. "But why the hell would somebody wanna kill Burden? Galler said he was a good man."

"Maybe," the sheriff replied. "Maybe not. Anyway, I went back to Galler's place but he still wasn't there."

"He won't be back," Raider offered.

Jenkins squinted at him. "How you know that?"

"Just a hunch."

The sheriff sighed. "Anyway, I also sent a wire to your agency first thing this mornin'. They said you was workin' here and that they would be obliged if I would help you."

"Thanks," Raider replied. "Now ever'body in town knows there's a Pinkerton here. Another Pinkerton t' look for Cynthia Galler."

"I did what I had to do," Jenkins said. "Here's your gun. You're free to go any time."

Raider pushed back from the empty plate. "Let me ask you somethin', Sheriff. How come you didn't go lookin' for that Galler girl?"

"It ain't none of my business," Jenkins replied. "Besides, I figured if there were four Pinks on the hunt, why should I look for her?"

Raider picked up his gun, spinning the cylinder. "You know anything 'bout that boy the girl was seein'?"

"Kreeger? Well, I never met him. Some said he come from Seattle, Washington. Said he used to go by the name of Hardy Morgan. But I never knowed that to be true."

Raider holstered the Colt. "What about the girl?"

"What about her?"

He eyed the hesitant lawman. "You holdin' somethin' back, Jenkins?"

"Never was one to talk mean about a lady."

"The lady bein' Cynthia Galler?"

Jenkins nodded.

"Well," Raider offered, "anythin' you got t' say will be 'tween you an' me. An' I figger you owe me after lockin' me up."

The sheriff sat down, leaning back in the chair. "Just between you and me, huh?"

"Won't get no farther."

"She was a pretty girl," the sheriff started. "But I didn't know her well. I just heard things."

"Like what?"

"For one, her and Kreeger were s'posed to be doin' things."

"What things?"

Jenkins blushed. "Things that you ain't s'posed to do until you get married. I don't know if her daddy knew, but I bet it broke his heart if he did. Course, people talk. They say she was the one who led Kreeger along, not the other way around."

Raider started for the door. "I gotta go have a look at Galler's place. You comin' with me?"

Jenkins shook his head. "Nope. I aim to stay out of this."

Raider thanked him.

"Pinkerton!"

Raider stopped at the door.

Jenkins pointed a finger at him. "I don't care who you are. If I catch you doin' anything wrong, I'll run you in as fast as anybody else. That gallows outside is for a man they're bringin' from Idaho Falls, but I'll string you up right beside him if you step out of line."

"I hear you, Sheriff. I hear you fine."

He left the office and started down the street with the sheriff's warning still fresh on his ears. But Raider figured it didn't really matter. He had a feeling that he wasn't going to be around Boise very much longer.

The early-summer sun was high overhead, warming the day, presenting plenty of light for Raider's investigation.

At the back door of the Galler house, he stood on the small porch, gazing down on the horse tracks that led away from Boise. Two horses, heading in the same direction as the mount of the man who had killed Harold Burden. Raider was sure that someone different had come for Robert Galler. After the killer had been shot at, he probably wouldn't double back for Galler.

What else? He stared at the tracks. The horse had not been there an hour earlier, when Raider had come in the back door to see Galler. So the other man had brought the second horse with him. He had come to get Galler.

Did Galler know he was coming?

Raider decided to look inside.

Stepping into the kitchen, he peered down at the floor. Small clumps of mud were interspaced as if someone had strode through the kitchen. The clumps ended on the carpet of Robert Galler's den. Raider took a pinch of the dirt and went back outside for a second, to compare it to the dirt in Galler's backyard. The clumps had not come from Galler's yard. The mud was thicker, darker. Galler's yard had sand in it.

Raider went back to the den.

So somebody had come in the back door, walked into Galler's den and then left with the mining man.

Raider gazed at the chair where Galler had been seated before. What was the redheaded man doing when the other person came in? Beside the chair was an ashtray with a half-smoked cigar in it. A glass of liquor rested beside the ashtray. Galler had been smoking, having a drink. Not expecting anybody.

A pile of papers had been placed on the seat of Galler's easy chair. He had probably been looking them over when the other person came in. Got up, put the papers down. That meant he didn't even sit in the chair again. Left his liquor and his cigar. Ran out in a hurry.

Raider glanced toward an empty coatrack across the room. Galler had taken the time to put on his coat and hat. So he probably wasn't taken by force. Maybe a gun was on him while he donned his coat. Maybe his kidnapper had told him to put on his hat slowly.

The big man saw only two possibilities. Either Galler was taken against his will, without force, or he went willingly with the small horseman. Raider's brow fretted. Why was he thinking the horseman had been small?

He looked at the mud tracks again. Small stride. Or maybe a careful stride. Stalking, looking for Galler, wielding a pistol.

Raider decided to go in the other direction and ask himself a question that needed to be figured. What if Galler had killed Harold Burden? What if he had discovered some sort of treachery on the part of his closest associate?

No. Galler was too old to scamper down a roof and drop to a horse. And he had seemed genuine in his defense of Burden.

Of course, that didn't mean that Galler was completely beyond suspicion.

Still, it appeared that a team had been in operation, pulling off a double ambush. One man had gone after Burden and the small man had gone after Galler. Comes in the back door, stealth in the hallway, brandishing a pistol or a scattergun. Galler's pale eyes bulge, his face goes white. The small man tells him to pick up his hat and coat. Galler doesn't fight. He leaves his drink and his cigar and goes with the small man.

Raider shook his head. He had imagined the whole thing in his head, like pictures in a book. Saw it, sensed it. Even if it wasn't true, he had—

The big man froze. His hand went to his Colt. He lifted it as the boots scuffled down the hall. Sheriff Jenkins went slack-jawed in the face of the gun bore.

"Pretty fast with that thing," Jenkins said.

Raider holstered the Colt. "Wouldn'ta hurt for you t' knock."

"Gotta talk to you, Pinkerton."

"Say it quick. I ain't sure I'm gonna be around here long."

Jenkins eyed him. "Where you goin'?"

"I ain't sure just yet," Raider replied. "Mebbe you can help me out on that. How 'bout it?"

Jenkins shrugged. "What makes you think I'm you're man?"

"Don't snow me, Jenkins. You're an on top o' the kettle 'round here. You had your eye on what's going on. So far you had the good sense t' stay outta it. You think it don't concern you as long as the other people of Boise ain't hurt by it."

Jenkins shook his head, grimacing. "I reckon you Pinks are as good as they say. You're right, big man, I've been watchin'. There's somethin' I shoulda told you back at the jailhouse, but I let it slide. Kinda got to botherin' me that I held back."

"Get it off your chest, boy."

Jenkins tipped back his wilting felt hat. "That Kreeger. I saw him going after the girl. But her daddy never came to me lookin' for anything. I reckon he went to Jimmy King while Jimmy was still sheriff."

"What happened t' Jimmy?"

"Never came back," the sheriff replied. "Rode out to look

for the Galler girl and we ain't seen hide nor hair of him yet."

"Damn, what the hell is goin' on?"

"I don't know." Jenkins sighed. "Anyway, like I said before, Kreeger was known to have used the name Hardy Morgan. I also found out that he was s'posed to be surveyin' for Mr. Galler, so I went to the assay office to see if Kreeger was registered. He wasn't. Neither was Hardy Morgan."

"Galler said that he never saw any of Kreeger's survey work. He prob'ly ain't a surveyor at all."

"He definitely ain't," the sheriff rejoined.

"Why'd you hold back?" Raider challenged.

Jenkins looked down at the floor. "I don't know. I didn't see that it mattered. And I figured you'd look it up yourself. Then I thought I might save you some time."

Raider eyed the penitent lawman. "Glad we're on the same side. Jimmy was a honest man, an' I hope you are. But you still don't seem too eager t' git this thing solved."

Jenkins sighed. "Way I see it, Raider, I ain't hired to protect these rich folks. They got their own way of doin' things. The town council don't seem to care if Cynthia Galler gets found. The way the good citizens of Boise see it, she got what she asked for. It ain't the first time some hot-kneed chippy got herself into a mess and run off with a drifter. And I can tell you that it won't be the last. Nope, Cindy Galler is already forgotten around here. People are thinkin' about statehood for this territory. That's what's on their minds."

Raider wanted to say that Boise might be judging Cindy Galler a little too harshly. A reputation built on rumors was a hateful thing. Raider had to ride through the rumors to the facts. But he decided not to challenge the sheriff. After all, Jenkins was cooperating.

"Where you think Galler went?" the big man asked.

Jenkins pointed north. "That way."

"Why?"

"That's where his mines are. And there's somethin' goin' on up there. I know it. You know it."

Raider frowned, gesturing toward Galler's wooden desk. "I wanna see for myself, Sheriff."

With Jenkins looking over his shoulder, Raider started to go through all of Galler's personal papers. The correspondence from Galler's creditors proved that the mining man had reached the end of the vein. He hadn't raised enough ore to pay for a tenth of what he owed.

The sheriff sucked air through his teeth. "Dang, you think a rich man don't have no problems!"

"Sure 'nough, Jenkins. I reckon Galler is poor 'nough for you t' start protectin' him now."

"That was a low blow, Pinkerton."

"That it was, Sheriff. That it was."

Raider unrolled a long map that had been drawn the month before. The map maker was a local man, somebody who could be seen in person. Raider searched for marks on the map.

"There," he said finally. "Cascade. That north o' here?"

Jenkins leaned over to look at the dot that had been circled in black. "Yep, it's north. I can tell you that's where Galler has his old mines."

"Any idea where he had his new digs? The ones that were no good?"

"Up near McCall," Jenkins replied. "There, it's on the map."

Raider traced his finger up to the small, uncircled dot. Tiny X marks were clustered northeast of McCall. The new digs, or at least the proposed locations for more silver mines.

"I reckon I'll be headin' that way," Raider said. "I coulda used a better night's sleep than I got in your jail."

"Sorry, Raider."

"Aw, you were just doin' your job. An' if I find out you're mixed up in any o' this, I'll go ahead an' do mine."

"I bet you will, big man. I bet you will."

Jenkins laughed.

Raider began to roll up the map.

"You goin' up there now?" the sheriff asked.

"Later," Raider replied.

"Well, where are you goin'?"

"T' see the map maker, Sheriff."

Jenkins said that made sense to him.

Raider hesitated, stopping as he turned away. The glint of glass over a picture had caught his eye. He took the frame off Galler's desk, holding it closer so he could study her face.

"This the Galler girl, Sheriff?"
Jenkins nodded. "Pretty, ain't she?"
Raider slipped the frame inside his vest. "It won't be missed."
The sheriff nodded his head in agreement.

CHAPTER TWELVE

The map maker remembered Hunt Kreeger. The handsome young man had come in to buy a map of central Idaho. It had to reach as far as McCall. The cartographer remembered the strange request that had come from the polite young man. Kreeger had asked him if he knew anything about surveying, or of any surveyors in the area.

"Of course I knew of one surveyor," the map maker went on. "I gave him the man's name but never heard any more about it."

So Kreeger had been wanting to cover his back, to hire somebody to do the work if Galler caught on that Kreeger wasn't really a surveyor.

Raider asked for the name of the surveyor but was told that the man had gone to Idaho Falls and would not be back for a month.

Raider then showed the map maker the picture of Cynthia Galler. He knew who she was but had never seen her in person. Raider asked if the man knew the late Harold Burden, but the map maker had never even heard of him.

"What's McCall like?" Raider asked.

The cartographer shrugged. "Dirty, what there is of it."

"That figgers."

"What?"

Raider tipped his hat and bade the man good day.

He headed for the general store. Best to lay in a few provisions if he was going up into the mountains. He'd also have to take a look at the mounts for sale in the livery. Maybe he could find one better than the gray.

The trail away from Burden's place was still fresh and Raider held to the notion that it would connect somewhere with the trail from Galler's house.

At least it was still summer in the mountainous northern regions of Idaho. White pines waved brightly in the breeze, with mountain bluebirds flitting between the boughs. Syringa was in bloom, along with mountain flowers that Raider could not identify. Perfect weather for trailing. Warm days, cool nights. But he had no way of knowing how close he was to the men who had killed Burden and kidnapped Galler—if Galler had been kidnapped.

As he had figured, the trail from Burden's place intersected the trail from Galler's house. Raider had followed the tracks until they disappeared on high, rocky ground. From there, the big man had held a steady northern gait, making for Cascade.

On the porch of the general store in Cascade, Raider met several local men who expounded on many topics when aided by a jug of corn liquor. Gradually Raider brought the subject around to Cynthia Galler. As a mountain zephyr stirred the noonday heat, everyone took a gander at the pretty, long-haired woman. Nobody remembered her, but several men thought they recognized the description of Hunt Kreeger—only that wasn't the name he had been using. Raider offered Kreeger's alias, Hardy Morgan, but nobody remembered the name.

They all knew of Robert Galler, the mining man. Some had worked for Galler before his operation had gone bust. They described him as a fair man, although they never liked the man who was working for Galler, Mr. Harold Burden. Raider told them of Burden's murder and of the danger that Galler might be in. They wished they could help, but none of them had seen Galler in a couple of months. Nor had they ever seen the Galler girl.

As Raider was slipping the picture back into his vest

pocket, one of the idlers offered the tale of the Blackfoot Indian ghost that roamed the hills looking for a bride. If Cynthia Galler was in the mountains, the spirit might have gotten her. The man then chose to rattle off a list of names, girls who had disappeared over the last few years.

Raider listened patiently, trying not to laugh. The old man made the story sound pretty convincing. Of course, Raider never believed in such things unless he saw them with his own eyes. And seeing it was half the task of explaining it. He had rooted out "evil spirits" before, usually to find that some flesh-and-blood man was behind the demon.

Gradually the men on the porch got around to asking Raider about his line of work. The big man replied that he was Cynthia Galler's second cousin from Boise, that he was a hunter most of the time but he was now looking for his kin that had disappeared. He thought they bought the story for the most part. He also wondered how long it would take for news of his arrival to spread through the mountains.

As Raider enjoyed a big plate of stew and bread, the men began to talk about Robert Galler's misfortunes. It was a shame that his mines had gone bust, a shame that the new mines at McCall had not panned out. Some of the other digs near McCall had rendered great strikes of silver ore. But it was a testimony to Galler's bad luck that he had come up empty.

The big man didn't say it, but he figured the key to the mystery of Galler's daughter—and the missing Pinkertons—lay in McCall, or at least in the vicinity.

One of the idlers asked about the Pinkertons who had been sent up to look for Cynthia Galler. Three of them had come through Cascade and as far as the man knew they had gone to McCall. The man asked if Raider was a Pinkerton. Raider asked back if he looked like a Pinkerton. The man said that he did not. Raider laughed in agreement.

When his mount was rested, he started north again.

Maybe it was the ghost story that made him ride on into the night. Raider kept a steady pace, saying to himself that he would stop and make camp soon. Build a fire, have a couple of pieces of jerky, get some sleep. But he never stopped. He went on until the sky began to grow blue overhead.

Low, yellow, billowing clouds soon closed in to prevent the daybreak from warming the mountains. The air stayed cool, moist. Raider figured he should be in McCall soon, if he hadn't strayed completely from the trail during the night. He listened to the thunder which never turned into rain.

He stopped at a clear, rocky creek to drink and to water his new mount. He had traded his gray gelding for a fine chestnut stallion. When the animal was ready to go again, he swung into the saddle, plodding north. How much farther could it be to McCall?

Around noon, he reached a signpost on the trail. It was a crude, slapdash sign that declared: "McCall, Five more miles. Don't try unless you mean it." But that wasn't what turned Raider's head. It was the sign underneath that one. It read: "Morgan Mines." And the arrow pointed northeast in the same direction as a second, sparsely traveled path.

Morgan. One of Hunt Kreeger's aliases. Morgan Mines. Raider climbed down and studied the sign more closely. The name *Morgan* had been painted over another name. Raider took his knife and scratched until he saw enough of the second name to know that it was *Galler* that had been painted over.

Well, at least he didn't have to go to McCall.

Best just to ride straight in. Pretend he was a miner looking for work. Play it close, safe. Keep eyes and ears open. Don't make a mistake. Don't wind up missing like the four men who had come before him.

The trail narrowed before it opened into the small canyon. A stream ran down the middle of the crevasse, flowing to the southeast. Above the stream rose a high cliff that stretched up as far as Raider could crane back his neck. The mining encampment was at the base of the cliff, serving the adit that appeared to be a pack rat hole about a hundred feet up the slope. A man on a rope hung suspended between the mine entrance and the ground. Another worker seemed to be pulling at the opposite end of the rope, hoisting his coworker toward the dig.

Raider halted the chestnut stallion, keeping to the shadows that fell from the rocky crags overhead. Best to take a good look first, before he went in. Check out the lay of the camp.

Two brown structures stood to the left of the man with the

rope. A tent was pitched on the floor of the canyon, a hundred yards east of the buildings. The rope line was the only way to get up to the dig. And the mining operation seemed to be in full swing.

Raider dismounted, leading the stallion behind some tall boulders that rested in the middle of the stream, breaking it into two rapids. Raider let his mount drink. After he had dunked his own head in the stream, he climbed onto the boulders and took another look at the encampment.

He had to consider a few important factors.

First, if Galler had been kidnapped, he would probably not be at the mining site. Maybe he was stashed in Cascade, or in some lonely mountain line shack. Kreeger had taken him and had painted his alias over the sign. Now it was Morgan Mines, open for business.

But why had Kreeger killed Burden? Maybe they were in league and Kreeger just plain wanted to cut Burden out of his share. Or maybe Burden had been on the level, had caught on to Kreeger and had paid for it.

He watched the adit for a while. A man came to the entrance of the mine and lowered a basket on the end of a rope. The ore. Silver, probably. Kreeger had done it right. Get the girl, sucker the father into thinking his new digs were dry. Then take it all in one good stroke.

How was Raider going to approach it? Ride in, ask for work, risk being identified.

There didn't seem to be too many men around. So far he had only seen the two who were working the mine. The tent was closed, motionless. Maybe he should wait until dark, poke around when everybody was asleep.

The chestnut snorted.

Raider looked back to see the animal lift its head. He didn't want it to drink too much. A horse with a bellyache wasn't any good for making quick getaways. He came back down the rocks to catch the horse's reins.

The chestnut reared.

"Damn it, boy, what's wrong with you?"

"He heard me, white man."

Raider glanced over his shoulder as the rifle lever clicked. A wiry, gray-haired Indian stepped toward him on moccasined feet. His face was brown and wrinkled. His spotted hands held a shiny Winchester that pointed straight at Raider's forehead.

The big man tried to smile. "Snuck up on me pretty good there."

The Indian's black eyes stared at his hands. "Your gun is slung pretty low. I think you're here to cause trouble."

Raider figured him to be Shoshone, although he was dressed more like a Cherokee: bright red shirt, sash, tanned leather pants. A red scarf was tied tightly over his head. Long, gray locks came out of the scarf.

Putting his palms to the sky, Raider said: "Hey, I'm just here t' look for work, Jasper. Ain't this a mine?"

If the old buck didn't buy it, just move the stallion between them and draw the Colt.

"My name ain't Jasper."

"Whatta they call you?"

The Indian eyed him carefully. "Red Bear. Whatta they call you?"

"Ray. Ray Weathers. You work for Mr. Morgan?"

"Whatta you know about Mr. Morgan?"

Raider shrugged. "His name is on the sign, ain't it?"

Red Bear nodded. "Yes, I reckon it is."

Raider grinned as wide as he could. "Red Bear, I'm gonna put my hands down. You can shoot me if you want, but I don't mean no harm."

"All right. But slow."

The big man moved slowly. "You're Shoshone, right?"

Red Bear said he was. He didn't seem to think Raider was so smart for guessing his tribe. It was an easy choice, what with most of his people up in Canada now.

Raider glanced back toward the mine. "You gonna take me to see Mr. Morgan? Or ain't he hirin'?"

"He's hirin'."

That made Raider hopeful. Now he had to pray that Robert Galler wasn't in camp to identify him. Somehow he felt the former owner of the mining claim was far away from this lonely ravine.

Red Bear turned toward the encampment. "Come on."

"You trust me enough to show your back?"

"I know you won't shoot me."

Raider fell in behind him. "How you know that?"

"Because you came here for another reason."

Raider decided not to ask him to elaborate on that statement. Old Indians could talk you around in circles sometimes. Best not to get involved.

"Bringin' that silver outta the mountain," Raider said as the man above dumped more rock into a basket.

"Not yet," was Red Bear's only reply.

They followed the stream back into the canyon. Raider caught a better view of the two shacks that rested on the left side of the dig. Nothing more than tin-roofed hovels. And behind the structures was the remuda of horses and mules that had undoubtedly packed in supplies for the camp.

"How much is Morgan payin'?" Raider asked.

"Not enough to make it matter."

The big man wasn't sure he liked the tone of Red Bear's voice, but he held his tongue. He had gained one ally or at least he had duped the enemy. Then he heard Red Bear call to Mr. Hardy Morgan and Raider got his first surprise.

Raider wasn't sure why he was taken aback by the appearance of Hardy Morgan, alias Hunt Kreeger. For some reason, Raider had been expecting a harder looking man, a razor-eyed weasel with a strong chin and broad hands. Somebody who could handle himself and a gun. But this version of Hardy Morgan wasn't much to look at, not from an outlaw standpoint.

Morgan—as Raider now began to think of him—came strutting toward them in a pale gray suit. He was thin, white-skinned. A straw hat protected his face from the sun. His walk wasn't manly and his handshake was limp. He didn't seem like the hellion that Raider was looking for.

"Hardy Morgan, mister—"

"Ray Weathers," Red Bear said.

Morgan smiled warmly at the Indian. "Good work, Red Bear. You culled me a miner out of the rocks." Morgan tossed the Shoshone a silver dollar.

Red Bear caught it and shrugged. "He told me he would give me a dollar if I went up to Cascade and found him a miner."

Raider nodded appreciatively. "He drew down on me t' git me t' come in here, Mr. Morgan. And he didn't haveta go all the way t' Cascade. I saw your sign on the trail an' d'cided I oughta take a chance."

"I don't care," Morgan replied. "Keep the dollar, Red Bear. Can you start to work tonight, Ray?"

The big man squinted at the dapper bandit, wondering why Morgan had become so generous. "T'night?"

"I want to work 'round the clock," Morgan replied. "Of course, if you can't handle the work—"

Raider shrugged. "Day, night. Don't matter t' me. Long as I get paid."

Morgan gestured to the Indian. "Red Bear, get him settled in the bunkhouse. He can start after dark." He turned and started toward the tent.

Raider called after him. "Thank you, sir. You know, I tried like the devil to get work in Boise but some boy name of Galler has almost gone outta bus'ness."

Morgan stopped in his tracks, wheeling to look over his shoulder. His eyes were bright green, expectant, like he was waiting to hear some satisfying piece of gossip. Raider didn't consider him much of a man, but he was the kind women sometimes liked. Clean and shiny, slicked-back blond hair, thin face and nose and lips. There was a hint of cruelty in his smile, just for the instant when he turned to face Raider.

"Bad news?" he asked.

Raider played dumb. "Didn't hear much more 'bout it. Just that he weren't hirin'. I got outta town when the sheriff came after me."

Morgan sighed, resuming his friendly expression. "Well, we shouldn't grieve too much over the misfortunes of others. We're sure to be there soon enough ourselves."

He went toward the tent.

Raider wasn't sure what to think. Morgan/Kreeger hadn't been at all what he had expected. But that didn't matter. Weasels would poke under a log until they got what they were after. The big Pinkerton from Arkansas planned to do the same damned thing.

"Gonna show me t' the bunkhouse, Red Bear?"

He turned around but the Indian was gone.

• • •

Raider felt the shadow behind him. He turned, looked back over his shoulder. Then he smiled. He didn't know what made him smile.

Then he felt the pain in his back, small like a prick from a turtle cactus. At first the pain didn't bother him. But then he realized that the dark shape had shot him. He couldn't understand why he had not heard the shot. Or why he could not smell the gunpowder.

And he fell. A long way, into darkness. Tumbling until he heard something snap. Was it his spine?

Raider sat up in the cool air of early evening. Sweat poured off him. He looked around the shabby bunkhouse, where he had been sleeping on the corn shuck mattress. It always took him a while to remember after he woke up, but it came back to him. He was at the mine, the dig that had been stolen by the man going as Morgan, the man who had probably kidnapped Cindy Galler and her father. He shook off the dream as he focused.

"You don't sleep very light."

Raider glanced up to see Red Bear coming at him from the shadows.

His hand moved quickly, sticking the Colt in the Shoshone's face.

Red Bear nodded as he sat in a rickety wooden chair. "I thought you'd be fast," he said matter-of-factly. "You look the kind."

Raider eased the Colt back into the holster that rested next to him on the mattress. "You always turn up like a spook, Red Bear?"

"I am a spook."

Raider leaned back on the mattress. "I bet you are."

"I know things."

The big man smiled. "Yeah? Like what?"

"You're not a miner," Red Bear offered.

Raider raised up on one elbow. "I'm not gonna let you make trouble for me, Injun."

"I coulda slit your throat in your sleep, cowboy."

Red Bear's lined faced lifted into a slack-skinned smile.

Raider leaned back again. "I guess you coulda. So what the hell you want from me, Red Bear?"

"Only what the buzzard wants from the mountain lion.

Leave enough for me when it's all over."

"Ain't gonna be nothin' left over. I'm just a honest miner, come here t' help Mr. Morgan. Glad he could give me some work."

Red Bear laughed. "He asked me to work for him."

"Why didn't you?"

"I'd never work for a white man. I don't have it in me. Besides, I don't like high places. I wouldn't want to ride up that rope."

Raider thought about the single line that would lift him to the adit high above. The entrance of the mine looked to be almost three hundred feet off the ground. He also knew what the work would be—hammer and chisel, cracking out pieces of the mountain's gut. His arms would ache afterward.

"You ever mined before?" Red Bear asked.

"Once. When I was a kid. What's he got here? Green spots or a whole vein?"

"Nothin' yet."

"Nothin' at all?"

"Nope."

Raider put his hands behind his head, staring up at the ceiling. Maybe the digs were worthless. But why would Morgan go after the Gallers if the mine was a bust? Even if Morgan hadn't found anything yet, he was counting on it. Betting on the next roll of the dice.

Red Bear was staring at him. "How long you been a lawman?"

Raider didn't flinch. "What makes you think I'm John Law?"

"Ah. You wear your gun low. And you ain't no gunslinger, not the kind that's out for hisself anyway."

"So that makes me law?"

Red Bear did not reply. He took a plug of tobacco out of his pocket and bit off a hunk. He held the plug toward Raider but the big man shook his head.

"Gotta tell you somethin'," the Shoshone said finally.

"I'm listenin'."

"You'll hear it sooner or later."

"Old man, are you gonna talk me t' death?"

"Ever hear of the shawmee?"

"You mean the Shawnee," Raider said, "it's a tribe o'—"

"No. The shawmee. Hell, don't feel bad that you ain't. It's local. This story about a Shoshone warrior that comes to claim his bride every spring."

Raider grinned. "Yeah? Live around here, does he?"

Red Bear grimaced, rolling the tobacco on his tongue. "He's dead, you horn toad. It's a spirit. A ghost."

"Yeah, reckon I heard 'bout that one. Only it was a Blackfoot warrior up in Montana."

The old man shrugged. "I wouldn't doubt it. But I wanted to tell you so you'd know. You'll find out when you start looking for the girl."

Raider got up quickly, taking several long strides until he was in the man's face. "What you know 'bout the girl?"

"She's here."

Raider shook his head, grinding his teeth. He hated it when old warriors like Red Bear ran him around the barnyard. He couldn't be sure how much the Shoshone really knew. Maybe he was pretending to know more than he did, trying to draw Raider out by insinuation, using his instincts to ferret out the truth.

"Gimme a name," the big man challenged.

"What kinda name?"

"A girl's name."

Red Bear laughed. "No. Just take my word for it. She's here."

"What's she look like?"

Red Bear pointed across the room. "Like that picture in your saddlebag."

Raider scowled at him. "Why you old mountain goat! You were lookin' through my stuff while I was sleepin'."

"Okay," the Indian offered. "I was. But I knew that there were others here, looking for that same girl."

Raider grabbed the cotton fabric of the old man's shirt, jerking him out of the chair with angry strength. "What the hell you know 'bout the others? I mean it, old man. Tell me what you know."

"Let go of me," Red Bear replied calmly, "and I'll take you to them."

"They're alive?"

"Please. Let go of me."

Raider dropped him back into the chair. "Look here, Red Bear, I ain't got nothin' agin you yet. But if you don't stop playin' games with me, I'm gonna haveta take it outta your hide."

The old man waved nonchalantly. "You won't have to hurt me. I'm on your side. Or as close to it as I can be. Like I said, I want you to leave some for me at the end."

"How many came lookin' for the girl?"

Red Bear held up five fingers.

Raider felt his stomach turning into a tumbleweed. "Are they still alive?"

Red Bear was pursing his lips to answer when the door to the bunkhouse swung open. Hardy Morgan stepped into the shadows. He leaned in the doorway, peering in at Raider.

"Time to go to work," he said.

Raider nodded to his new boss. "Yeah, just as soon as I—"

He turned back to look at Red Bear. The chair was empty. He thought he heard the old man scuffling away outside. He had gone through the window. More spry than he appeared. The wrinkled warrior had actually crept up on Raider and had rifled through his saddlebag. How much did Red Bear really know? Maybe he had put it together with lucky guesswork.

"Are you coming to work?" Morgan asked again.

Raider nodded, reaching for his shirt. "Yeah, boss, I reckon I am. Sorry, it takes me a while t' wake up."

"Me too."

Morgan smiled and talked pleasantly to the big man as they walked toward the hoist that lifted the miners to the adit. A brawny, rough-faced Shoshone worked the wheel that cranked up the rope. He was lowering another tired-looking digger to the ground.

Morgan put his hand on Raider's shoulder. "Now all I want you to do is dig out the same hole that this man was working on. If you see a wide spot of gray, come to the entrance and wave to us."

Raider looked up the steep, dark cliff. "How am I gonna see up there?"

"Lanterns. You can hold one and wave."

"Anybody else workin' with me?"

"The mine's not big enough," Morgan replied. "Not yet.

Just give me an honest night's work. I'll pay you two dollars a day, with a five dollar bonus if you find a vein."

Raider agreed to that, thinking the man must be well-heeled to throw around bonuses. Or at least he figured to be rich pretty soon. Wealth that he had taken from Robert Galler. Now all Raider had to do was prove it.

CHAPTER THIRTEEN

Raider slipped the harness around his torso and buckled the strap.

The Shoshone was looking at him, his rough hands on the wheel that lifted the makeshift seat.

Raider nodded to the Indian, who tensed and started to pull the big man up along the sheer wall of the cliff. What the hell had made Morgan start to dig so high up? Maybe he was smarter than anybody figured.

He felt the harness tighten into his body. The straps caught a little, pulling the hair on the back of his legs. His boots bumped the rocky face of the mountain. Raider had to hang on to the rope above him to keep his balance.

As he rose, he thought of Red Bear again. His eyes strained to the northeast, peering into the darkness. Somewhere that old Indian was hiding in the shadows, having a good laugh. Did Red Bear really know where Raider's four colleagues and Sheriff Jimmy King had gone so mysteriously? Or was he just taunting the big man from Arkansas?

As the rope drew him toward the sky, he gazed out at a glow that seemed to rise in the distance. Cascade? It seemed logical that any of the four agents who had preceded him had gone into Cascade. Raider would have to hit town sooner or later. If Morgan had the Gallers, he was probably keeping them in Cascade. Nowhere to really hide them at the mine, unless they were somewhere in the rocks. Somehow Raider felt they weren't.

His feet scuffled onto a high ledge at the entrance to the mine. The adit was just big enough for him to step into without bumping his head. He had to balance on the lip of the mine, trying to get out of the harness. His boot heel dug into a rock that broke loose. His legs fell out from under him.

Raider grabbed for purchase as he went over the side. Sharp knees of stone dug into his chest and stomach. His legs dangled freely beneath him. White knuckles. Gasping for air. Rush of energy that always came when he was close to dying.

His hands filled with stone. Raider's arms ached as he pulled himself back onto the ledge. He sat down as best he could and wriggled the harness off his body. Maybe it hadn't been such a good idea to ride into Morgan's camp and look for work. He was stuck with it though.

At least he'd have his days free to poke around, to find Red Bear again.

Slowly regaining his balance, he entered the mine. A hammer and chisel awaited him. He'd have to do some work to make it look good. So far the hole wasn't even fifteen feet into the mountain.

A low-burning oil lamp flickered inside, throwing spooky shadows in the enclosure. Raider saw the chisel marks in the rock. Just as Red Bear had said, there were no signs of silver.

The hammer didn't feel right in his hand. A gun was more to his liking. And he preferred a knife to the chisel. Still, he had signed on as a miner and he had to fill the bill at least for a couple of days.

Balancing the blade of the chisel against the rock, he struck one blow with the hammer. Bits of stone flew off the wall, some of them striking his face. He had to wipe a speck out of his eye.

All the time he kept thinking that he was going to wring Red Bear's neck when he finally got a hold on the old Shoshone.

For some reason, Raider took to the work with a vengeance. He hammered all night, dumping his waste off the cliff. He came down just before morning to find Hardy Morgan waiting for him.

"You nearly doubled the other man's work load," Morgan said proudly. "Did you find anything?"

Raider pushed past him, heading for the bunkhouse. "I didn't wave, did I?"

The other miner was getting into the harness.

Morgan put his hands on the lapels of his coat. "Well, good work anyway. I'm sure you've made things easier for us."

Raider strode through the cool air of daybreak, trying to remember when he had been so tired. He just wanted to sleep for a couple of hours before he started looking around. He planned to search the immediate area first. His trip into Cascade might have to wait a day or two, till he was paid. After all, it wouldn't seem out of line for a hardworking miner to want to spend a little of his pay. And what better place to do it than Cascade? Morgan wouldn't suspect a thing.

As Raider hit the first rickety step of the bunkhouse, he heard light footsteps scuffling across the floor. He went through the front door and looked toward his gear.

Nothing there.

The breeze blew through the open window.

Raider went to the rough casement, peering up toward the slopes to the north. He thought he saw the bright hue of Red Bear's shirt against the rocks. He strained to see the old man waving at him.

How the hell had he gotten way up there?

Unless it had been someone else after Raider's gear. He checked his saddlebag. The picture of Cindy Galler was missing. He went back to the window to see Red Bear moving through the rocks. Best to follow him now, even if Raider was dog tired.

As he was saddling the chestnut stallion in the shed behind the bunkhouse, Hardy Morgan approached again with his friendly face all drawn up in a smile. Raider still wasn't sure what to think of the dapper gentleman. Morgan seemed pretty calm for a man who had stolen a mine and kidnapped two people.

"Going somewhere?" he asked.

Raider nodded. "Thought I might try to find a patch of woods. Mebbe shoot a mule deer." He patted the Winchester on his saddle's sling ring. "Got me a rifle." He hesitated, wondering what Morgan was going to do.

"Good hunting," the man said. "I'm going back to sleep."

Morgan started for the white tent that served as his headquarters.

Raider swung into the saddle, thinking that Morgan didn't seem so dangerous. Neither did a rattler till you stepped on it. Then it bit you deep and hard, needling that venom into your veins. It took a leg or maybe your life.

But where the hell was Morgan's firepower? Two miners and a Shoshone strongman. He hadn't even asked if Raider knew how to use a gun.

A call echoed down from the slopes.

Raider looked up to see Red Bear waving at him again. The big man turned the chestnut upward. He'd ride as far the animal would take him and then he would walk if he had to. He just wanted to corral Red Bear and get some answers out of the wrinkled old man.

Red Bear was leading him a merry chase.

At first, Raider couldn't figure out how the spry old bird was doing it. He seemed to always be there, staring down at Raider from some high perch on the mountain. Then he would laugh, his grating Shoshone howl rolling through the air like the cry of a screech owl. Raider would take a bead, follow him, and then find that he was gone again, moved on to the next spot up the trail.

The big man from Arkansas had to admit that he was spooked a little. Red Bear appeared to have unnatural powers. How else would he have been able to soar up the mountain so fast? Like a damned redskinned leprechaun, that's what he was.

But Raider stayed after him, even when he had to climb down from his saddle and lead his horse. He told himself to use his head. Figure out how the old man was doing it. Don't give in to superstition. Examine the trail, look for signs, make sense out of it.

On a patch of softer ground, he saw the small hoofprints. A burro; that was it. A smaller mount would be able to stay ahead of him with ease. A damned donkey could scurry through the hills without a hitch. Short little legs carrying Red

Bear to the next rock. Raider had to smile. The old boy knew what he was doing.

But where did Red Bear think he was going? And why was he so set on drawing Raider away from the mine encampment? Maybe the old Indian really knew what had happened to the four Pinkertons who had come looking for Cynthia Galler. Or maybe it was just a ruse, a way of leading Raider straight into an ambush.

The big man paused on the trail, gazing skyward as the morning sun made its way toward afternoon. Too hot for this early in the summer. He tried to remember the date but found that he was not even sure of the month, much less the date or the day of the week. He took a long drink from the canteen that he carried on his saddle. The water was too warm but it wet his dry mouth and throat.

After he poured some water into his hat so the horse could drink, he found some dried meat in his saddlebags and ate a few bites. Had to keep up his strength. Working in the mines all night had not helped. But there was no time to catch a nap, not if he was going to chase the Shoshone.

Red Bear made it easier. As the day became hotter, the trail became more apparent. He had turned southeast, away from the higher slopes. Raider peered down into a valley that was covered with brush and trees. Woodlands. At least there would be some shade.

Leading his horse, he began the descent. Red Bear's laughter urged him on. The old man was definitely in the trees, darting between the shadows. When Raider entered the forest, he found a piece of red cloth tied to a branch. Another marker hung about a hundred yards farther up the trail. Red Bear was climbing, going higher. Raider took a deep, tired breath and thought about it for a minute, finally deciding to follow the old man. At least for another hour or so. It was beginning to look like Raider was not going to catch Red Bear. Of course, there was always the possibility that Red Bear might catch him.

He started slowly, cautiously, through the dim shadows between the thin trees.

"He's a Pinkerton."

"Are you sure?"

A nod of the head.

A sigh. "Too bad."

A smile. "Word came from McCall. He denied it, but I was able to confirm it from you-know-who."

"How is he?"

A shrug. "He'll get over it."

Another sigh. "This one won't be as easy as the others. He looks a lot tougher."

A scowl. "Well, if you're not up to it—"

A weak, apologetic smile. "I didn't say that. I just said that it was going to be harder. That last one was easy. The hardest part was getting him to the spot where all the others were buried."

A triumphant smile. "But you did it remarkably well."

"Thank you."

"And you won't let me down on this one."

"I haven't let you down yet."

"No, you haven't."

Eyes turning to the mountains. "He's out there. But I think I can find him."

"I'll get ready."

"I'll bring the heavy rifle. I don't want to take a chance with this one. Not as big as he is."

A furtive turn, a raised eyebrow. "I do believe you're afraid of him."

"No, just a bit wary. He seems to be the lucky type."

"How so?"

A shrug. "He got this far. I wouldn't have known about him if you hadn't told me."

"That's why we work together. A team."

Another smile. "Yes. And we'll have all that we've dreamed of."

"Yes, we will."

The two Pinkerton killers went about their chore, plotting the end of the big man with the black eyes.

Raider was just about played out. The stallion didn't have much left either. The big man stopped beside a stream that ran through the bottom of a narrow, wooded ravine. Red Bear had gone up and then down again. Raider peered up the sides of the crevice. The damned sun beat down on everything, baking the countryside as well as his brain.

His head throbbed and his throat was dry again. He dipped his head in the stream, finding the water to be cool and sweet. The chestnut nuzzled in right beside him. Raider washed the back of his neck and then dipped his face again. He needed to sleep, even if it was just for a couple of hours.

Rising to his feet, he looked upward, along the sides of the ravine. The trees provided plenty of places for bushwhackers. But so far he had not seen any signs that didn't belong to Red Bear. Raider could not remember when someone had eluded him so easily. Maybe it was best just to give up, to get back to the mine and rest before before his next shift. Morgan would be expecting him to return. Best to follow through with the masquerade, as long as it suited his purposes.

When he considered the legalities of the situation, he realized that he had Morgan dead to rights. Ownership of the claim on the mine could be proven. Lawmen and judges could be brought in if Morgan really had stolen the mine from Galler. Still, Raider wanted to find his missing colleagues and the two kidnap victims first. Which meant that chasing Red Bear had suddenly become unimportant. Best just to get back to camp.

Raider reached for the reins of the stallion. The animal snorted and shied away. It didn't want to move for a while. Raider felt the same way. So he tied the animal in the shade and found a spot for himself. He stretched out with his Colt resting on his belly.

"Light sleeper," he said to himself, remembering Red Bear's cutting remark. "Shit."

He closed his eyes, knowing that he would wake at the slightest sound.

But when he finally came to again, Red Bear was sitting on the ledge above him, laughing like a Montana maniac.

He chased the old Indian again. It was probably a mistake. The big man had slept away most of the day, so he might be late getting back to work at the mine. He could always tell Morgan that he got lost.

Red Bear had been perched on a high ledge that jutted out from the forest. When Raider arrived at the flat piece of rock, he saw that Red Bear's burro had been tied to the stump of a dead tree. Raider walked to the edge of the precipice and gazed back down into a deep pool of the stream he had been drinking from. A long drop. And the chestnut was still tied in the shade. He had come up the mountain on foot, following a narrow, rocky path.

The pool swirled cold and blue at the bottom of the ravine.

Raider felt fresh again, ready to go.

He gazed up at the sky, which was as blue as the pool below him. Maybe three hours of daylight left. Time enough for a quick look around then back to the camp. He would be a little late, but Morgan would just have to live with it.

"You're mighty slow for a lawman."

Raider wheeled quickly, his hand dropping for his gun. The Colt's barrel glinted in the bright sun. Red Bear laughed when he saw the cold stare of the gun's bore.

"You won't need that," the old Shoshone offered. "I don't even have a weapon."

Raider held tight to his gun. "You got me confused with somebody who gives a damn, Red Bear. I'm gonna shoot you just for playin' games with me. Ridin' that damned burro all over creation."

"Good animal. You'd never catch a white man ridin' a burro. White men don't have any sense. Look at you. You followed me all the way up here. Why'd you do that?"

Raider sighed, lowering the Colt. "I don't know. I reckoned that you might know somethin'."

"I do. And it's time to show you."

Red Bear started to turn away.

Raider caught him with an arm around the neck, slipping the muzzle of the Colt into the small of the old man's back. "Walk slow, honcho. You're gonna lead the way, in case there's anybody up there waitin' for me. Let 'em shoot you first."

Red Bear laughed again. "A good idea. But you don't need it. The only thing waiting for you at the top of this rise is a shovel."

Raider didn't bother to try to figure out the Indian's cryptic comment. He just pushed him forward, back into the trees. The ground became steeper as they climbed.

"Don't blame me for what you find," Red Bear offered as

they trudged between the narrow tree trunks. "I didn't do it."

"Do what?"

"You'll see. We're here now."

Raider stopped, balancing on the slope. He scanned the area but saw nothing out of the ordinary. Except—there seemed to be a fresh mound of soft earth in the middle of a clearing, like it had just been turned over. Raider let go of Red Bear.

"You stay close," he warned.

The Shoshone shrugged. "Maybe."

Raider eyed him. "You know, you speak the white man's tongue pretty good, for someone who hates white men."

"I suppose."

"And you were quick to take that dollar from Morgan when I first rode into camp. Then you tell me you'd never work for a white man."

Red Bear pointed toward the soft earth. "Better get to work, before the varmints get in here and dig them up."

The big man squinted at the brown, wrinkled face. "You better not be involved in this, boy, or I'll shoot you sure as hell."

"Oh, I'm involved. But not like you think. Ain't I helpin' you? Ain't I brought you up here on this mountain?"

"I still don't trust you."

"I ain't asked you to trust me," Red Bear replied. "Now pick up your shovel and dig."

Raider turned to see the small spade leaning against a tree. He suddenly felt a churning in his gut. He wasn't sure he wanted to know what lay beneath the ground. He looked at Red Bear again.

The Indian shook his head. "Oh no. I ain't diggin'. If you want to know what's goin' on, you'll have to do it yourself."

Raider gestured with the Colt. "I could make you do it."

"No you couldn't."

He sighed, holstering the weapon. "What am I gonna find there, Red Bear? Go on, tell me."

"Those four men that came lookin' for the girl."

"Shit!"

"Okay, don't believe me."

Red Bear turned to walk away.

"Hey," Raider called, "I didn't appreciate you stealin' the picture o' the girl. I want you t' give it back."

"Didn't do it," the old man replied. "But I'm sure you'll find the one who did. Just dig. You'll be late for work if you don't."

"Where you goin'?"

Red Bear looked over his shoulder and smiled. "Don't worry, I'll be right here. I won't go far. And I won't let anybody sneak up on you. Except me. But you won't hear that anyway."

He laughed that eerie chortle again.

Raider thought about stopping him but then realized he'd have to shoot Red Bear to get him to stay. He finally had to figure that the old man really didn't mean him any harm. Not just now anyway.

So he picked up the spade and started to dig in the fresh earth. There was too damned much physical labor involved in this case. First the mine and now the infernal digging. He'd have to— The smell hit him.

Raider had to step back for a moment to wrap a bandanna around his nose. He knew what had been buried in the hole. The odor of a dead man was very familiar to him. As he started to dig again, he had to wonder if Red Bear was telling the truth about the missing Pinkertons and the sheriff.

The first body was dressed in a brown suit, the same kind that agent Stanton always wore.

He had to pull it into the light.

Goddamn smell.

Partially decayed.

Lift by the clothes so nothing would fall off.

How long had the body been in the ground?

Quite a while.

The suit was as rotten as the body. Raider could not recognize the face. He prayed it wasn't Stanton. There was only one way to tell. Stanton always carried a wallet in his coat pocket. His Pinkerton credentials would have been in the wallet.

Raider found the leather billfold and opened it. A long, worm-like creature fell onto the ground. Raider had to stop himself from gagging. He had to think of the poor bastard who was in the ground. Make himself look at the wallet.

Stanton's Pinkerton papers were soiled and tattered, but Raider could still read them.

He turned away from the body, looking into the trees. "Red Bear! Git down here. I mean it."

No reply.

"That son of a bitch."

His heart was pounding. He wanted to hurt somebody, the man who was responsible for Stanton's death. But there was only the soft rustling of the trees to mock him.

He looked back at Stanton. Best to try to keep his head. Put old Will back in the ground. He had been a good agent. Now he was dead. Raider had to rethink his plan before he ended up the same way.

That poor bastard.

Raider dragged the body back and put it in the grave again. The other four were probably buried beneath Stanton, or at least close by. Stanton was the last one to die, so his grave was the freshest. As Raider covered the dead man, he had to wonder why the ground around the grave had been so soft. Stanton appeared to have been in the ground for a long time. Maybe Red Bear had been poking around himself.

The damned thing was getting stranger and stranger.

But it didn't matter. Raider had to stay on top of things. He patted down the earth, thinking that the grave was too high up for coyotes or cougars. At least old Stanton would rest easy and not be disturbed.

What next? Get down to his mount. Maybe ride to Cascade to send a wire. He had already decided not to go back to the mining camp. Even if Morgan did not seem to be a dangerous adversary, he was still mean enough to take care of four Pinkertons and a sheriff.

As he came down out of the trees, Raider paused at the ledge for a moment to look for his mount. The stallion was still tied where he had left it. At least Red Bear hadn't seen fit to torment him further.

He turned away, gazing back into the trees again, wondering if he would be able to find the other four graves. Damn it all, how was he going to tell Wagner that four agents were all dead and buried? Maybe three of them were still alive. Right. Just get to Cascade, send the wire and wait for help. This was one time when the big man would request assistance.

Stanton. Raider shook his head. Stanton had been almost as good as Doc Weatherbee. He wasn't the kind to let somebody get the drop on him. Wasn't that how it happened though? Sooner or later some bastard with a gun sneaked up behind you and—he stopped, listening to the breeze.

Was something moving in the forest?

"Red Bear?"

He heard footsteps.

His hand filled with the Colt.

"Come down here, you—"

His eyes bulged when he saw it. A whitish shape gliding down the slope. And there was an Indian, not Red Bear, but another Shoshone in full battle dress. The big man hesitated. What the hell was it?

The white shape became clearer.

"Hey, what are you doin' up there?"

But the shape did not seem to hear him.

He squinted, trying to make it out. Was it a girl? And the Indian was right behind her. He wanted to fire the Colt but he wasn't sure what he was shooting at.

He was going to call again but another voice echoed through the trees.

"Lawman. Look out!"

It sounded like Red Bear.

Raider was turning to run when the rifle exploded. He felt a pain in his head. Then everything went black. He staggered a few steps and then he seemed to be floating. Or falling. It didn't matter much. Just before he passed out, he figured he was dead.

"You think he's dead?"

The Pinkerton killers were standing on the ledge where Raider had fallen into the pool of water below. They were straining to look for the body. They could not see it.

"No one could have survived that fall. Not even a lucky man."

A sigh. "I hope not. Send the Indian to look for him."

"Red Bear?"

"No. I want that old fool killed next time we see him. He almost warned the damn Pinkerton in time to save him."

They were silent for a moment.

"He couldn't have survived that head shot. And it's a long fall. He's dead. I'm sure of it."

Uncertainty in the voice. "I hope so."

"You were afraid of him. Weren't you?"

"You weren't?"

"I'm not afraid of anything."

"No, I suppose you're not."

"Send the Indian to look for him. Have the body brought to us."

"I'll do that."

But for some reason, the body of the big, black-eyed man never turned up.

CHAPTER FOURTEEN

William Wagner stepped slowly along Fifth Avenue, taking his time in the heat of the summer sun. His right hand held a damp handkerchief that went repeatedly to his forehead, dabbing away the beads of perspiration. Wagner hated the heat. He could not remember the last time it had been so torrid in Chicago, particularly so early in the year.

When he arrived at the office of the Pinkerton National Detective Agency, Wagner immediately instructed his clerks to open every window in the place. If they were lucky, they'd get a breeze off the lake. Nothing much to be done except ride it out and keep the handkerchief handy.

"William!"

Wagner turned to see Allan Pinkerton motioning to him.

"William, come into my office at once."

Wagner ignored the imperious tone in his superior's voice. He chalked it up to the heat. It made people short-tempered.

"William, I can't get anything done in this swelter!"

Wagner nodded. "Nor can I."

"Look at my desk, covered with work."

"Mine is just as cluttered," Wagner replied.

Pinkerton sat down and sighed deeply. "I sent for a pitcher of lemonade. Would you be wantin' some?"

"Of course."

Pinkerton fanned himself with a thin sheaf of papers. "This business in Nebraska seems to drag on."

"Are the crops still being burned?"

Pinkerton nodded. "I've got four men on it, although this seems like something for that big galoot Raider."

Wagner flinched when he heard the name. "You know that's impossible. He's still in Idaho."

"Any word from him?"

"Not since that business in Boise. I daresay the whole territory know he's there now. But it was the only way I could get that local sheriff to release him."

Pinkerton scoffed at the thought. "He's more likely to get in trouble than a cat in a field full of mice."

Yes, Wagner thought, but if you put Raider in a field full of mice, he'd probably melt his Colt trying to shoot them all.

Where were such notions coming from? he wondered.

The damned heat.

Pinkerton exhaled. "Raider's the fifth man we've sent after that Galler woman. What in the name of all that's holy has happened to her? And who's doin' away with all our men?"

Wagner wanted to say that was what they sent Raider to find out, but he held his tongue. Pinkerton just needed to blow off steam. He knew that there was nothing they could do about Raider, which made the situation all the more frustrating.

"William, can we contact the state government? Get the governor to do something? Somebody in Idaho must owe us a favor."

Wagner shook his head. "Not that I know of. Besides, Idaho isn't a state. It's still a territory, which means that the government isn't all that efficient yet."

"There's nobody to help us?"

Wagner thought about it for a moment. "Well, I suppose I could send a wire to the marshal's office. Although he probably won't be much help."

"What about that sheriff?"

Wagner shrugged. "A chance. But he's probably glad to be rid of Raider and I doubt he'll go looking for him."

"Bah!"

The lemonade arrived. Both men tried to quench their

thirsts. Sweat popped out on Pinkerton's face, running down to his starched collar.

Wagner knew what was bothering his boss because the same thing was bothering him. They really didn't need Raider in Nebraska, but they would have felt a lot better if they had known the big man was alive. Losing five agents, including two of their best troubleshooters, was not something that happened with any regularity, not to the Pinkerton National Detective Agency.

"We need rain," Pinkerton said.

Wagner nodded. "It would surely help."

"Not a cloud in the sky."

"No, sir."

Pinkerton sighed. "Wc'll wait another month. If we haven't heard from Raider, I want ten of our best men on the case."

"What about Nebraska?"

"To blazes with Nebraska! I want our men found, do you understand?"

Wagner said he understood perfectly.

One month. Until then, the big man from Arkansas was on his own.

CHAPTER FIFTEEN

There was darkness for a long time. Swirling, heady nightmares came after the darkness. There was falling and then coldness. Sense of movement. Gasping for air. Crawling.

Then the darkness seemed to be replaced by light. White light all around the big man. He was aware of the brightness even with his eyes closed. And when he finally opened them, the glare was overwhelming.

Voices surrounded him, though he could not be sure how many of them there were. They faded in and out, like his own sensibilities. His eyes would open but he would feel them closing again. Coolness on his forehead. Somebody touching his face with a moist cloth.

"Looks like he's gonna be with us a while," a man said.

Someone held a cup of water to his lips. He drank, finding that he was parched. He tried to hold the cup but a gentle touch assured him that he was not that strong yet.

He strained his eyes, squinting.

Her face came into focus. Pretty, soft features. Blue eyes, blonde hair hanging down on her forehead. She wore a white dress.

He tried to speak but found that his voice was not working right.

The woman leaned down, trying to listen.

She laughed when she understood what he was saying.

"What's he want?" the man asked.

"He's asking if he's in heaven," the woman replied.

The man chortled. "That's a good one."

She dabbed his face with the cloth again. "No, you're not in heaven. You're in Idaho. Some say that's close to heaven, others say it's closer to hell. But you're still alive."

"Now Cassie, watch your language. This man could be offended by such talk. He could be a preacher."

"He's no preacher," the girl replied. "And if you were as concerned about our dig as you are my language, we might be a lot better off."

"Hush up, daughter!"

She hushed, but not before she gave her father a rebellious look.

The man moved closer to the bed, leaning over to stare at the big man's head. "Take that bandage off."

Gentle hands unwrapped the cloth from the big man's skull.

The man examined a wound on the right side, near the hairline. "Not as deep as I thought. Better put some more salve on it."

The hands dabbed something on the wound. It felt warm on the tender tissue. The hands wrapped a new bandage around the big man's skull.

As the girl worked, her father looked into the big man's eyes. "Clear," he said. "Look at that. Never seen eyes like that. Black as the night."

The girl stared into his black eyes. "He's not a bad person."

"How do you know?"

"I just do."

The father eyed his daughter, shaking his head. "Now don't get no fool notions about this one, Cassie. He ain't gonna take the place of your dead husband. You can't—"

"Oh, hush," she said impatiently. "I ain't gettin' no notions. I just want to make sure he stays alive."

The father lit a match, torching the bowl of a corncob pipe. "He's gonna live. But that wound was made by a bullet, Cassie. Somebody was shootin' at him and I don't want you to take a shine to him till we know *why* they was shootin' at him. You hear me?"

The girl nodded.

The father leaned in again. "Can you tell me why someone was shootin' at you, partner?"

The big man wanted to say something but his mind was blank. So he closed his eyes again, feeling weak and distant. He slept for a long time before everything became clear again.

Heat seemed to be closing in on him, forcing him to open his eyes.

The girl in white was hovering over him when he awakened.

"You were shaking," she said. "Having a dream. Do you remember what you were dreaming about?"

He moved his head, indicating that he did not remember.

"I've got some soup for you," she said, lifting a spoon toward his mouth. "Here; it's only broth."

The big man took the salty liquid, finishing the bowl as she fed him.

"You've got to get your strength back," she said.

He stirred, trying to sit up. His head spun so he fell back onto the pillow. His arms and legs did not respond. He closed his eyes again.

"Sleep," she said softly.

He was aware of her lips as she kissed him on the cheek.

The next morning, he awakened with a clear head. His eyes were able to focus on the room around him. He was lying in a modest cabin that had been fashioned from logs. The bed felt good on his back. Was it a feather mattress?

He tried to sit up again. His head was light but he managed to rest his back against the wall. Something told him not to stand up so he stayed where he was until the girl came in.

"Well, you look to be better," she said, smiling.

For the first time, he was aware of her features. Kind, smooth face. Light skin, full lips, prominent cheekbones. Her hands were rough, like she had been doing some kind of hard work.

"How about some coffee?" she asked.

The big man felt the word forming on his lips. "Whiskey."

She frowned. "Oh. Well, let me get my father. He doesn't allow me to know where he keeps his jug."

She left, returning with the older man after a while.

He told her to go outside, to leave them alone.

When she had made her exit, her father pulled a clay jug from beneath a loose board in the floor. "Don't let that girl take drink," he said to the big man. "Ain't proper. Don't take much myself. Only once in a while I like a nip."

He poured a cupful and handed it to the man in bed.

His hands were stronger. He sipped the burning liquid that immediately made his head throb. When he grimaced, the older man shook his head.

"Not too much, now."

The throbbing was replaced by a gentle glow that spread over his body.

The girl stuck her head in. "Is he better?"

A sigh from the father. "Dadburned females is too nosy. Yes, he's better. But it seems strange to me that he'd ask for whiskey first thing."

"Maybe he knows what's good for him," she replied.

Her father could see the look in his daughter's eyes. She had hopes for the black-eyed man. Hopes that nothing could quell.

"I'm Cassie Lonnegan," she said. "This is my father. His name is Homer Lonnegan."

The big man nodded.

Homer Lonnegan stared at his houseguest. "Well, I reckon it's about time you told us who you are."

"Yes," the big man said.

His face slacked. His head went blank. Nervous trembling on his lips.

"Well?" Homer Lonnegan asked. "Who are you?"

A tear rolled out of the big man's eye. "I don't know," he said. "I just don't know."

As his strength returned, it began to bother Raider that he had no memory of anything prior to his appearance in the Lonnegan household. Every day he would awaken to a hot breakfast prepared by Cassie Lonnegan. She attended him like a good wife, making sure that he was fed, that the dressing on his wound was changed. He kept hoping that the next morning would bring clarity, but his recollections did not return.

In the evenings, he would get out of bed to sit in a chair

beside Homer Lonnegan. They'd share the jug and talk.

According to the older gentleman, they had found the big man lying on the bank of the creek. Or rather, Cassie had found him. She had been on her daily trek for water when she spotted him lying in the sand.

"Did I have anything on me that might say who I am?" Raider asked.

Homer shook his head. "Nothin' that I could find. Cassie searched a ways up the creek bed, but she said she didn't find a thing."

The big man sighed, feeling weak again. "I better git back in bed."

Homer stopped him. "We did find this," he said, opening his hand.

Raider looked blankly at the money. "Is it mine?"

"Was in your pockets," Lonnegan replied.

"Keep it. For all the trouble I caused you."

"Thanks. Minin' ain't been too good to us lately. Wasn't so bad before the fever took Cassie's husband. Had enough to last us for a while. But since I'm workin' the dig by myself—"

Raider stood up. Something had flashed through his head. The image of a hammer and chisel. He was standing in the dark, pounding on a wall of rock.

"You okay?" Homer asked.

"Mining," the big man said. "Mebbe I was a miner. Mebbe I—"

He teetered, reeling with confusion and pain.

Homer Lonnegan jumped up to catch his arm, leading him back to bed.

Cassie appeared at the door to the bedroom. "Is he all right?"

Raider stretched out on the feather mattress.

The old man waved his daughter away. "Just a dizzy spell. He'll be okay after he rests a while."

The girl nervously bit her knuckle. "I don't want him to die, Papa. Please don't let him die."

Lonnegan led his daughter back into the other room.

Raider put his head on the pillow, staring up at the logs in the ceiling. The image of a dark mine would not leave his head. And nothing else would come to him. He just lay there, wondering who the hell he was, wishing he could remember his own name.

After the first week, Raider's strength came back to him. He was able to get out of bed every morning, to have breakfast with the girl and her father. He had to admit that he was beginning to like Cassie. She was cheerful, radiant, helpful. A good woman.

The old man had a fine disposition as well. He was friendly, talkative—but not enough to be bothersome—and he liked to crack off a good joke now and then. Once in a while he would fart at the dinner table, only to make some remark about having a bullfrog in his pocket. And he would go off to dig the mine each day, taking his pick, chisel, and hammer along with him. He also slung a holster over his shoulder, carrying an ancient Navy Colt to work with him. Couldn't be too careful, he said, not with all the copperheads and other varmints about.

Two-legged varmints, the big man thought.

A pain shot through his forehead. He remembered dark men with evil faces. Why? Where had they come from? He couldn't put names with the faces but they were there, swirling in his head.

"Are you okay?" Cassie asked him, her hand on his shoulder.

Raider looked up to see the old man glaring at him.

He brushed Cassie's hand away. "Yeah, I'm okay. Mebbe I oughta go work the mine t'day with your daddy. Gittin' kinda restless 'round here."

Homer smiled at him, nodding appreciatively. "Welcome all the help I can get, stranger."

The girl glared at her father. "We can't keep callin' him stranger, Papa."

Homer agreed that it wasn't proper. "What do you want us to call you, partner?"

The big man shrugged. "Don't reckon it rightly matters."

"How about Bill?" Cassie suggested.

Homer eyed her. "Cassie, that was your husband's name."

She lowered her face. "Sorry, I—"

"Bill is fine," Raider said. "If that's what she wants."

Cassie smiled. "Don't you two be late for dinner, now."

Raider followed the old man out of the house. The sun was bright and hot on his head. He unwrapped the white dressing that covered his wound.

Homer Lonnegan stared at the gash on Raider's skull. "You were lucky, boy. Whoever shot you just missed. One more inch and you wouldn'ta had much of a head left."

Raider frowned, trying to recall.

"Somethin'?"

"No. Nothin'. How's this look?" He pointed to the wound.

Homer shrugged. "Seen men die from less. You're one tough piece of meat, partner."

"Mebbe. Where's this mine?"

Homer pointed east. Raider peered at the beauty of the ravine where they were homesteaded. Nice creek, a few trees, and some brush. Blue sky overhead. Had he been here before?

"Stranger?"

He turned back to the older man. "Yeah?"

"Cassie's got some fool notion in her head that God sent you to replace her husband. But I don't want you gettin' the wrong idea. From the looks of you, you seem to be a man who's used to trouble. And I don't need no trouble. You understand me?"

Raider put his hand on the man's shoulder. "I understand, sir. You saved my hide an' I won't b'tray you by sparkin' your daughter. Now come on, let's go work that mine. Mebbe somethin' will come back t' me."

But it didn't.

They worked hard all day, chiseling into the mountain. The labor helped to heal Raider's aches, although he became dizzy a couple of times. He huffed and grunted, wishing that something—anything—would come back to him. It was only at the end of the day that something happened to change his outlook. A bizarre occurrence. And it involved the old Navy Colt that hung over Homer Lonnegan's shoulder.

Cassie called them to dinner in the late afternoon.

Homer put down his chisel and hammer, picking up the gun belt that carried the Navy. He stopped for a moment to regard their progress. He nodded, patting Raider on the back.

"Maybe you were a miner, Blackie."

Raider dropped his mining tools. "Why'd you call me that?"

Homer shrugged. "I don't know. Black hair, black eyes. Don't really want to call you Bill. Why? You remember somethin'?"

He shook his head. "No. Nothin'. Seems like the name Blackie oughta mean somethin' t' me. But it don't."

"Come on, let's go eat dinner."

"Sure."

They started for the entrance. Homer Lonnegan went on about how he would have already found a good vein if he had had Raider to work with him all along. A big man with a strong back could be a real help in mining, he said. It took strong arms too, what with all the chiseling.

"You know, Blackie, I—"

He was almost to the opening in the rock when the copperhead slithered toward him. The snake drew back to strike at Lonnegan's leg. It missed the first time, getting the loose cloth of his pants.

Lonnegan leaped back, almost knocking Raider down. He drew the Colt from the holster, thumbing the hammer, trying to take aim with trembling hands. Two more snakes came up behind the first one.

"Damned nest of them," Lonnegan said.

He fired once but missed. All three reptiles drew back to strike. Homer tried to take aim again.

Reflexively, without any conscious thought, Raider grabbed the gun from Lonnegan's hand. He fanned the hammer, discharging three shots. The heads of all three snakes exploded. When a fourth serpent crawled into view, another burst from the Colt took off its head. The long, brown bodies wriggled out what was left of their lives.

Smoke wafted in the mine.

Raider stood there blankly, holding the gun loosely in his hand.

Lonnegan stared wide-eyed at the big man. "Partner, somethin' tells me you ain't a miner. Not with shootin' like that."

Raider just stepped over the dead nest of copperheads and started for the house.

• • •

Raider didn't say much through dinner. Nor did Homer Lonnegan. Cassie served them with the usual note of cheer in her manner. She went on about how much the big man had been a help to her father. She didn't even seem to care when neither man responded to her prating.

When her father was done, he pushed away from the table. "Think I'll go outside for a while. Maybe take my jug. You comin', Blackie?"

Raider felt a twinge of pain in his forehead. Why did that damned name sound so familiar? He saw the image of a uniform, the figure of a brawny man with large hands. Had the man hit him? Had they fought?

Cassie Lonnegan put her hand on his shoulder. "You all right?"

He nodded. "Come on, Homer. I could use a snort." Had he always been a drinking man?

Outside, they built a fire. The air was cool in the ravine. Lonnegan took a pull off the jug and offered it to Raider.

The corn whiskey made some of the pain go away. But it couldn't stop the dull ache inside him. The ache that came from not knowing who he really was.

"You might be a gunslinger," Lonnegan offered.

Raider sighed. "You think so?"

Lonnegan shook his head. "You're fast enough. But somehow your nature don't seem to fit a gunfighter. Course, that bump on your noggin mighta made you forget all the men you killed. Coulda changed you."

That made sense to the big man.

"You were sure quick with that gun," Lonnegan went on. "Never seen a man shoot so fast. Got all four of 'em and only took one shot each."

Raider leaned back, staring into the fire. "It just seemed t' come natural t' me."

Lonnegan exhaled a long, raspy, exhausted breath. "If I didn't like you so much, I'd think you were sent by one of them other minin' companies to run me out."

Raider looked at him. "Which minin' companies?"

"Ah, you know."

"No, I don't."

Lonnegan shrugged. "Well, there's Continental Silver, Oskow Mines, and that Galler."

Raider felt the pain again. "Give me some more of that corn."

Lonnegan passed the jug. He struck a match, torching his pipe, keeping one eye on the big man. The stranger with no memory seemed to know how to drink and shoot, habits that were not relegated to a decent, Christian man.

"What were those names again?" Raider asked.

"Continental, Oskow, Galler."

"The last one," he said. "Don't sound right."

Lonnegan shrugged. "Maybe 'cause a man name of Morgan done took it over."

Morgan. Raider sat up straight. Morgan. Why did that sound so familiar? He tried to recall, but his head began to ache.

"You okay, big 'un?"

Raider nodded. "Yeah, I reckon. This business has got me addled."

Lonnegan stood up. "Well, I'm gonna turn in. Listen, that fool daughter of mine can't seem to shake these notions of hers—"

"I won't bother her."

"That's not the point," Lonnegan said. "I'm worried about her botherin' you. If she does, I can't hold you responsible. She's a big girl. Gonna be twenty-four next month. Got over the death of her husband better than I could have expected. But since you come, she's got herself all worked up."

"Women can get like that."

Lonnegan eyed him. "So you know about women too."

The big man shrugged. "I s'pose I do."

A defeated sigh from Lonnegan. "I'm goin' to bed, Blackie. If you—"

"Blackie! I was in Canada. O'Malley. He—"

But it faded as quickly as it came. He only had the name. No face, no way to identify a man who had once called him Blackie.

"I'll leave the jug," Lonnegan offered. "Try not to kill it."

"I won't, Homer. I won't."

The old gent went into the house, to his bed in the loft.

Raider sat staring into the fire, wondering if he would ever know his own name. The jug helped a little. But it wasn't enough.

An hour passed before he heard the footsteps behind him.

Cassie Lonnegan came up to sit beside him.

"You helped my father today," she said softly.

Raider sighed. "Yeah. But I owe him. I owe both o' you."

She asked for a pull from the jug.

The big man hesitated.

"I know where he keeps it," she replied. "I steal a nip now and then. In this country you need somethin' once in a while. It's hard country. Not like Iowa. That's where we came from."

"Why didn't you keep your husband's name after he died?" Raider asked.

Cassie looked into the fire. "Didn't seem like the right thing to do," she replied. "He was gone. I just—"

She started to cry.

Raider curled an arm around her. Cassie fell onto his chest, sobbing. He had to fight the surge that went through his body when he smelled her hair. Somehow he felt that he wasn't good enough for a woman like Cassie. What made him think it?

Her face turned upward, her eyes sparkled in the light from the fire. "Kiss me," she entreated.

"No."

"Just a kiss. Please."

The damned smell of her hair. Her full lips were parted. Just a kiss. Would it really hurt?

"What about your paw?" he asked.

"He's snoring. Please. Kiss me."

So he kissed her, thinking it would stop there.

But it didn't. She touched him, the way a woman knows how to touch a man when she's had some experience. He touched her back. Her breasts were firm and round. Her hand rubbed his crotch.

"I want it," she said.

"Cassie—"

"Please, Bill."

"I'm not Bill."

She looked into his eyes. "I was a married woman. I got used to it. I want it again."

"Cassie, I cain't marry you."

"I don't want you to marry me, I want you to—please—"

He wondered how he would be able to look the old man in the face.

Cassie began to lift her dress. She guided Raider's hand to the wetness between her legs. Then she went to work on his fly.

"You're bigger than Bill," she said.

"Right here?" he asked.

She spread out on the ground. "Right here."

He took it slow. He wanted to be tender, loving. Something told him that her husband had been that way.

She gasped when he penetrated her. "Don't hurt me."

He didn't hurt her.

They were sweating by the time he felt his discharge rising. He pulled out and shot on her stomach. Cassie gazed up at him, asking him why he did it. He told her that she didn't need any babies. And though he didn't say it, he knew he didn't need a wife.

He rolled off her, wondering if he already had a child somewhere.

She snuggled against him. "I love you, Bill."

"I'm not Bill, honey. You cain't think I am. I might be somebody that's wanted by the law."

"You're not."

"How d' you know that?"

She kissed his cheek. "I just know."

Raider peered up at the dark sky, almost wishing he was Bill. It would have made things a lot simpler. Who the hell was he?

"What are you going to do?" Cassie asked.

He shrugged. "I don't know. I reckon I'll help your daddy at the mine for a while. T'pay him back. Honey, don't tell him 'bout this. Please."

"I won't."

"I better go in t' bed," he offered.

"Sleep with me tonight."

"No. Your daddy would have a fit. Besides, I gotta be fresh t'morrow. Minin' is hard work."

"Papa's not working tomorrow. He's goin' into Cascade to pick up supplies."

Raider sat up. Cascade. That rang a bell, even if the pealing wasn't so loud. Maybe somebody in Cascade knew him.

Maybe he had business there at one time. It sure seemed familiar.

"What is it?" Cassie asked.

He rose to his feet. "Nothin'. Just—well, I think I better go into Cascade with your paw."

"Good," Cassie replied. "I'm goin' too. We got a couple of mules. Paw keeps them in a corral down the creek a ways. We can all go together."

The big man wondered if that was such a good idea, but he finally decided not to talk her out of it. Something told him she would not relent. And he didn't feel like a confrontation, not on this night anyway.

"Cassie—what we done t'night—I ain't sure it was right. And if your paw was t' find out—"

She peered up at him with those hopeful eyes. "He won't. I promise. And it won't happen again. Not till after we're married."

"I ain't asked you yet," he said blankly.

"Don't worry; you will."

She got up and kissed him on the cheek and then headed back to her house.

Raider watched her go.

When she was inside, he sat down and stared into the fire again, wondering what kind of man he really was.

CHAPTER SIXTEEN

Raider had to hand it to Homer Lonnegan. The old boy was smart. His mule corral was proof of his intelligence. Lonnegan had penned his mongrels in a small indentation in the rock, about a hundred yards up the creek. He only needed three saplings to keep them captive. The rest of the corral was steep, solid rock. A cougar would have had trouble getting in.

Water trickled down into the enclosure, pooling for the strong pair of animals that brayed when they heard Lonnegan approaching. Homer had a bale of hay set up on a counterbalanced lever. As the mules ate, the bale became lighter, sinking lower and lower with each bite.

"Got the hay from a fellow in Cascade," Lonnegan said as he lifted the saplings from the entrance. "If it's danglin' over 'em, they'll only eat what they need. It's too much work for 'em to eat if they have to raise their heads up. I give 'em oats twice a week and they nibble the moss on the rocks."

Raider nodded appreciatively, staring at the gray mules. Where had he seen a mule before? All over, probably. Mules were common in Arkansas.

Arkansas?

"No, the mules were in Arizona," he said out loud. "Screaming. The mule is dead. Somebody had to shoot it."

Lonnegan was staring at him. "You all right?"

Raider wiped sweat from his brow. It was only after sunrise and already the day was simmering. Why the hell was he in Idaho?

"Blackie?"

"I'm still kickin', Homer. I just thought o' somethin'. Mebbe I'll be able t' put it t'gether in a while."

Lonnegan began to rub his chin, glancing sideways at the big man. "Son, there's somethin' I'd like to ask of you before we go into Cascade."

Raider tipped back the old felt hat that Lonnegan had given him. "I'm listenin', Homer."

"I want you to wear my gun."

The big man sighed. "That might not be a bad idea, Homer. I gotta tell you, I felt right comfortable with that pistol in my hand."

Lonnegan eyed him, like he was sizing Raider up. "You look like a miner. Those clothes of mine are small on you."

"I'm used to it."

"You are?"

Raider shook off the dizziness that tried to spin his head around. "Let's get to Cascade, Homer. You can give me that gun too."

"Maybe somebody will know you in Cascade," the old miner offered.

"That's what I'm afraid of."

They bridled the mules and led them toward the house.

Raider pointed to the dig as they passed it. "What makes you think there's silver in there?"

Lonnegan gestured to the adit. "I already found one small pocket. Came to almost five hundred dollars."

Raider whistled.

"Ain't as much as it seems," Lonnegan replied. "I had to build this house. And I've had to feed us. Since my son-in-law died, I ain't been able to dig as much. But I know a big vein is somewhere in there. I studied on it. I've got to keep workin' it."

"I'll help you, Homer."

"I hope so, partner. I sure hope so."

Cassie was waiting for them. She and her father rode on the same mule. Raider climbed up on the back of the other one, riding bareback. As the animal began to plod foreward, the big man decided that he probably hated mules and riding without a saddle.

"A fine morning, isn't it, Raider?"

Cassie had called from behind.

Raider turned on the mule and looked at her. "What did you say?"

"I said, it's good the morning isn't grayer."

He saw himself giving money to a woman.

Lonnegan eased beside him. "We better go, Blackie. I want to get back here before dark."

The mules fell in side by side, braying as they started along the trail.

"I slept like a rock," Cassie offered, tossing Raider a wink.

He saw himself with her in the firelight, but it now seemed fuzzy, like all of his other vague memories. As if it had happened to somebody else. Old Lonnegan didn't seem to be any the wiser.

So he just stayed in line, following the man and his daughter. Cassie kept looking back at him, smiling. She had found him lying on the bank of the creek. After someone had shot him. Maybe she knew more than she let on.

He shook his head. Was he really suspicious by nature, or just cautious? He took in the world around him, smelling the air, gazing out across acres of vast expanse. It all seemed real enough. But where the hell did he fit in?

They kept on until midday.

Lonnegan reined up and pointed into the distance. "Cascade."

Raider rode up beside him, peering toward the grimy buildings in the distance. "Don't look like much."

"It ain't."

Lonnegan reached into a saddlebag that was hanging over his mule's withers. "Here, just like we said."

The old Navy Colt shone in the sun.

Raider took the weapon and strapped it around his waist.

"I cleaned it for you," Lonnegan said. "All six rounds are full up. I reckon you might need it more than me."

Cassie was biting her knuckle. "Papa, he doesn't need that."

"Hush up, daughter." Then, back to Raider. "Son, I think

you ought to ride in after us. I know you've been a help to me, but I don't want to be seen with you. No offense."

"None taken," the big man replied. "Makes sense, at least until I find out who I am."

"Good luck, boy."

Lonnegan spurred his mule toward the path that led down to Cascade.

Cassie looked back at Raider. "Wait, Papa. I want to tell him something."

"Hush up, daughter."

Cassie was still protesting as they hurried out of earshot.

Raider figured she wanted to say something sweet. Although the expression on her face had seemed almost frightened. Maybe she was the girl he should marry. Work the mine with— The thought struck him: marriage. He had lost something and it was all because of marriage. But what had he lost?

"Damn it all."

He spurred the mule, following Lonnegan.

Maybe the answers could be rounded up in Cascade.

Cascade was hot, steamy, smelly, and dirty. The dogs in the street were ugly, the signs on the stores painted sloppily by hand. Probably there weren't ten structures in the whole settlement and most of them seemed to be falling down. The big man was sure he had never been there before.

His mule's hooves stirred dust in the lone avenue of the mountain town. Raider's entrance was noted. Necks strained, curtains were pulled away from windows. A face loomed out at him and for a moment he focused on the image in a picture frame. But the curtain dropped and the woman backed away from the casement. Had she looked familiar? Maybe he had been in Cascade at one time.

The saloon was pretty ratty. Raider tied up the mule and went through the swinging doors. Five or six gray faces turned to regard him as he entered. One man stood up. Raider glared at him, watching his hands. The man hurried out of the place, running along the street.

The other barflies went back to their business.

Raider stepped up to the rough-hewn bar. A smallish man asked his pleasure, commenting on the merits of a local beer.

Raider nodded, studying the barkeeper's face. Nothing familiar about him.

"Somethin' wrong, stranger?" the barkeeper asked.

"You ever seen me afore?"

The barkeeper shook his head. "Nope, can't say as I have."

Raider leaned forward. "Take a good look."

The barkeeper backed away a little. "I said I ain't. Are you loco, mister?"

"Sorry, pardner. Just get my beer."

Raider turned toward the other patrons of the saloon. "How about it, boys? Anybody tell me who I am, I'll give you a dollar."

They grumbled, but nobody spoke up.

Raider was bluffing. He didn't have a dollar. He didn't even have a nickel to pay for the beer.

The barkeeper put the mug on the counter. "Five cents."

"Run a count for me."

"Sure."

Raider watched as the little man went back to his business. He seemed to be afraid of the tall stranger. Raider caught a glimpse of himself in a mirror behind the bar. The face was his all right. Rugged, scarred, tight-skinned, tanned. Who did that face belong to?

In the same mirror, he saw the doors swing open behind him. Two men came through and stopped. One of them was the man who had left earlier. He had returned with a second man who wore a Remington low on his leg.

"You!" the second man said.

Raider turned to them, squaring his shoulders.

The Remington man was not pointing with his gun hand. His fingers tickled the butt of the Colt. Angry, bearded face. Dirty, like the town.

"How do?" Raider offered with a friendly smile.

His hand had fallen next to the Navy.

Why wasn't he afraid?

Did he fight like this all the time?

It seemed so natural.

"I'm gonna draw on you," the Remington man said.

"No need for that, pardner. If you know me, I'd just as soon you tell me who I am. That way I won't have t' kill you."

Did he always talk like that?

The first man backed away from his partner. "I don't want no part of him, Esky."

Esky looked a little nervous himself. But he wasn't about to back off. "I warned you, mister. Now I'm gonna do it."

Raider's eyes narrowed. "Who am I, you bastard? Tell me!"

But the bearded man wasn't in the mood for talking. He started to draw the Remington. But Raider was a whole lot faster. He had pumped two slugs into the man's chest before the Remington was halfway out of the holster.

Esky staggered forward, falling facedown onto the planked floor. His revolver went off in its holster. Raider hesitated, seeing if anyone else wanted to try him. They didn't.

He took one step toward the door before a man with a badge entered, his gun drawn.

Raider froze with the Navy in hand.

The sheriff motioned with the barrel of a Peacemaker. "Drop it, boy."

"Esky came in to draw on him!" someone cried.

"Yeah, that's right!" another voice called.

A frown on the lawman's weathered face. "Esky Pilot?"

"That's him."

"Yeah, Esky came in to draw on this stranger," the barkeeper said. "The stranger was just defendin' himself. Esky even drew first."

"I still want him to holster up," the sheriff said. "Go on."

Raider eased the Navy into his holster. Something about dealing with a lawman, he thought. Had he been a sheriff himself? He seemed to remember not liking sheriffs. He wondered if this one was going to hang him for killing the man.

The law officer holstered his own weapon. "Well, that's it," he said with a tone that almost sounded like relief. "The last Pilot brother is dead. I reckon my job is goin' to be a little easier."

He looked at Raider. "Stranger, I got to thank you. If these boys said you was just defendin' yourself, then that's good enough for me. What truck did Pilot have with you anyway?"

Raider shrugged. "Don't rightly know. I was hopin' you might be able t' tell me, Sheriff. Or maybe you can ask this man here." He pointed to the weak-faced man who had run to get Pilot after Raider entered the saloon.

"I don't know," the man said nervously. "Esky just said if I ever saw a tall man with black eyes that I should come and get him. He never told me what he wanted with you."

Raider looked at the lawman. "How 'bout it, Sheriff? Any notion as to why this boy wanted t' kill me?"

The sheriff rubbed his chin. "Well, Esky did have three brothers. One of them was sent off to prison, Esky killed one hisself, and the last one was killed in this very saloon. Funny, him and Esky dyin' in the same place."

The big man sighed deeply. "Pilot. It don't sound familiar."

"Scum of the territory," the sheriff replied. "Won't never get statehood as long as this kind is here."

Raider took off his hat and moved closer to the sheriff. "Look at me! Ain't you never seen me afore? Don't you know me?"

A baffled expression from the lawman. "I—hey, take it easy, boy."

To the men in the bar: "Damn it all, don't somebody in here know who the hell I am?"

They just gaped at him.

Raider slapped the hat against his leg. "I cain't remember. I don't know who I am. An' nobody will tell me!"

"Let me through!" a female voice cried.

Somebody tried to push through the rubberneckers who had gathered outside the saloon.

"Let her come," the sheriff said.

Cassie burst into the barroom, gasping when she saw the body of Esky Pilot. She put her hands over her mouth and backed into Raider. He wrapped his arms around her shoulders, pulling her close.

Cassie turned, burying her face in his chest. "I almost got you killed," she sobbed. "I'm sorry."

Raider looked at the sheriff. "Can I go?"

The lawman nodded. "I might ask you to sign a paper."

Papers. Reports. He had something to do with reports. And telegraph messages. Lots of paper. He hated signing things, especially after men were killed. Had he killed a lot of men?

"I'm out at Lonnegan's mine," the big man replied. "I'll

sign anything you want." Best to go along. He had done it before. But for whom?

"Take her out of here," the sheriff said.

He led Cassie back to the general store, where her father was loading the mule. Lonnegan frowned. "Cassie, what the devil were you doin'?"

"There was shootin'," Raider said. "Didn't you hear it?"

Lonnegan nodded. "Yeah, I heard it, but I didn't think it was none of my business. Are you all right, Cassie?"

She nodded. "Raider had to kill a man and it was all my fault."

The father gaped at his daughter. "What're you sayin'?"

"I did it," she said. "I was selfish. I wanted him for myself. And when he woke up and didn't know who he was, I decided I wasn't gonna tell him. Not until he remembered, anyway. But now I got to."

Raider pushed her away from him, glaring at her. "That's the second time you called me Raider. What d' you know, girl?"

"I'll show you," she said, wiping her eyes. "When we get home. I'll take you to where I found you. You'll see."

"Let's get started then," the big man said.

Lonnegan replied that he needed to load the other mule.

"No," Raider said, "Cassie and me are ridin' back right now. Buy another mule if you have to. I'll work it off in the mine."

Lonnegan shook his head defeatedly. "Hell, partner, if you want it that bad, then go."

By the time Raider and Cassie returned to the ravine, there was barely enough light left to find the valuables that Cassie had hidden.

She led him to the hole in the rocks where she had stashed his saddlebags and his gun. He hoisted the rusty Colt. It felt good in his hand. The Winchester was rusting too. He'd have to clean them. He was a man who took care of his guns.

The chestnut stallion was stashed near the hole in the rocks. Raider's saddle was there as well. Cassie had been feeding the horse so it was healthy and ready to run. He turned to stare at her.

Cassie lowered her head. "I know you think what I done

was wrong. When I found you, I saw that you were alive. I knew you had floated down the creek, so I walked up for a while till I found your horse. I guess I was thinkin' that if you lost ever'thing, you might stay with me and Papa. Then when you didn't remember—I'm sorry, Raider."

"Where'd you get that name?" he asked.

She pointed to the saddlebags. "Them papers in there. They say you're some kind of agent."

Raider dug into the saddlebags but he couldn't read the papers in the dim light. Best to go back to the cabin. He could put the stallion in Lonnegan's mule corral. His heart was pounding. The girl had held back the answers, but now they were in his hand.

"I hope you can forgive me," she said dolefully.

He could see that she was genuinely in pain. "Aw, Cassie, don't worry. You ain't hurt nobody."

"What about that man in the saloon?"

"Somebody woulda killed him sooner or later," the big man replied. "B'sides, you gave your paw the money you found on me. Didn't you?"

"Not really. I just forgot to check your pockets."

He put a hand on her shoulder. "Don't fret, honey. Who knows what woulda happened if you showed me all this stuff a lot earlier? I know you were actin' in your own behalf, but you didn't do nothin' that any other woman wouldn'ta done in your place."

"Really?"

"Sure. I seen a lot worse done by women in the name of love."

Had he really?

She sniffled a little.

Then they heard her father calling, his voice echoing through the dusk, calling them to the cabin.

Lonnegan leaned over the dinner table, leveling a disapproving finger at his daughter. "It was terrible what you done, Cassie. Terrible!"

The dutiful daughter began to cry again.

Raider grimaced at Lonnegan. "Don't be so hard on her, Homer. It don't matter none. Not now."

"You coulda been killed in Cascade."

"Mebbe."

Raider handed Lonnegan the papers he had found in the saddlebag.

Lonnegan read by candlelight, nodding. "Pinkerton, huh? Known as Raider."

The big man sighed. "That's what it looks like, Homer. But that's all I could find. And I still cain't say I r'member what a Pinkerton agent is. Or that I am one."

"Kinda like a troubleshooter," Lonnegan replied. "Some say they burn the houses of innocent people, but you don't seem to be that kind."

"It's a kettle that won't boil," Raider said. "All I know is that I'm good with a gun, I'm suspicious by nature, and I'm s'posed t' be some kinda half-assed lawman."

"Pinkertons are detectives!" Cassie interjected. "Raider looks more like a saddle tramp."

Raider smiled.

Lonnegan frowned at them. "Are you two gonna get married?"

Cassie lowered her eyes. "It's up to him."

The big man started to say "No!" out of reflex, but something stopped him. Maybe this would be the place to end the trail. A pretty little wife, a mountain full of silver. How could he miss? It was probably better than being a Pinkerton agent. Whatever that was!

"We might just get hitched, Homer."

Had he really said it?

Cassie brightened in a hurry. "You mean it?"

The old man smiled. "Well, glory be."

"Let me think on it," Raider offered, hedging a little.

"Blackie, you take all the time you like."

Cassie kissed him on the cheek.

It felt good to be with them. Almost like home. Unfortunately, it wouldn't be like that for long.

"He's still alive."

Nodding triumphantly. "I told you he was tougher than the others."

"Those dirt claimers must have found him."

"He's dangerous."

A glare from narrow eyes. "Don't you think I know that? If you had shot straighter—"

"This bickering doesn't do us any good."

"I'll bet that old Shoshone helped him. Haven't you been able to find him?"

"No. Not yet. He hasn't been around. He probably knows that I'm looking for him."

A sigh. "Everything was going so good before that big bastard came along. Now what are we going to do?"

"Kill him."

"Again? I hope you don't miss this time."

"I won't. I've taken care of the matter. It seems as though Esky Pilot has several cousins who aren't too happy about his demise. For the right sum of money, they'll dispose of the Pinkerton."

An angry glare. "Spending more money."

"Don't worry. It's necessary."

"Not if you had shot straight."

"I said don't worry. There are four Pilot cousins. The Pinkerton won't have a chance."

"You said he was lucky."

"Not anymore."

CHAPTER SEVENTEEN

A couple of days later, Raider awakened to a noise outside the cabin window. Reflexively, he reached for the Colt that he had taken to hanging on the bedpost. The gun was now well-oiled, the cylinder spun smoothly as he thumbed back the hammer. Cramping in his gun hand. The work in the mine had him aching all over.

Easing out of bed, he stole past Cassie Lonnegan who was sleeping peacefully on the kitchen floor. Her upturned face was so beautiful. Maybe he would marry her after all. Homer Lonnegan had not been pressuring him for an answer. Probably the old man just wanted Raider to stay on and work the mine. Raider. What kind of name was that for a man?

Outside, in the cool air of morning, he saw the red-shirted man who stood on tiptoes, trying to peer into the window. Raider slipped up behind him and put the bore of the gun on his neck. The old Indian froze.

"Don't think 'bout movin'," the big man said.

Red Bear nodded appreciatively. "Good mornin'. You're gettin' to be a lot sneakier. I didn't think you had it in you."

Raider spun him around, peering into the lined face. "You know me?"

Red Bear squinted at the tall Pinkerton. "Sure I do. You know me too. Don't you remember?"

"Nope."

A disbelieving look from the Shoshone. "You chased me over half of creation. I was on the burro. I warned you, right before you were shot."

Raider turned his head so Red Bear could see the scar. "You know who did this to me?"

"Not exactly. But I can guess."

He raised the Colt to Red Bear's nose. "Then who? Tell me!"

"You ever hear of a man named Morgan?"

"The miner?"

The Indian nodded. "You were in his camp, minin' for him."

"That's a lie."

Red Bear shrugged. "I took you there myself. But if you don't want to believe me—"

He lowered the Colt. "I ain't no miner."

"I knew that all along."

"You did, huh? Well then, mebbe you can tell me what I really am. Go on, let's hear it."

"You're a Pinkerton, just like the papers said. I got them out of your saddlebag while you were asleep at Morgan's."

Raider scowled at the old Shoshone. "You seem t' know a lot 'bout me. But I don't know a damned thing 'bout you."

Red Bear squinted, his face slacking into a frown. "No need to play this game, Pinkerton. You know who I am."

"It was the slug that hit my head," Raider offered. "It made me forgit ever'thin'. Even now, after I seen those papers, I still don't know who I am. Anything you could tell me would be a big help."

"Then it's true," Red Bear said. "You really don't remember nothin' about the things I showed you."

"What? What did you show me?"

A sigh from the old man. "This isn't goin' to be easy. I reckon it would just be best to take you back to where it all happened."

Raider's eyes narrowed. "You mean you were there when I got shot?"

"Yeah, I—"

Raising the Colt again. "You bastard. You're probably the one who shot me. I oughta—"

"No, it was them! Not me. I tried to warn you. I called out. Don't you remember? If I hadn't spoken, you wouldn't have moved and the bullet would have hit you square. You fell off the cliff, into the water. That's what saved you."

"How do I know you ain't lyin'?"

"I came back to help you again," Red Bear said. "Word got around about a tall man with black eyes who killed the last Pilot brother. Said you left Cascade with these dirt claimers."

"Watch how you talk about the Lonnegans!"

"Okay, okay," Red Bear offered. "I'm sorry. If you don't want my help, just say so."

"No," the big man replied. "I want it. But you gotta deal square with me. Understand?"

As Red Bear was nodding, Cassie Lonnegan came around the corner.

"Raider?" She hesitated when she saw the Colt. "Is everything all right? Are you okay?"

The big man smiled and nodded. "Yeah, honey. This is just an ol' friend o' mine."

Her blue eyes peered at the old man. "Red Bear? Is that you?"

"It's me, Cassie."

Raider eyed him suspiciously. "How you know her?"

"He sells honey and wild onions to us sometimes," Cassie offered.

"Yeah," Red Bear rejoined. "I sell honey and wild onions to them sometimes. That good enough for you?"

Cassie smiled. "Papa offered him a job working in the mine but he says he won't work for a white man."

Something clicked in Raider's head. He heard the old Indian's voice as he said the same thing. He shook it off but he had to wonder if he was close to remembering.

"You want some breakfast, Red Bear?" Cassie asked.

"Why, I'd love some, Miss Cassie. If you don't—"

"No breakfast," Raider said. "Not yet."

Cassie frowned. "Why not?"

"'Cause this boy knows somethin' 'bout me an' I aim t' have him tell me afore we do anything else."

"But—"

"No, Cassie. This is important. He says he can take me back t' the place where I was shot. Mebbe it'll make me remember."

Tears welled up in the girl's eyes. "I don't want you to remember, Raider. You'll leave us if you remember."

The big man felt helpless in the wake of her tears, but he knew he had to find the truth. "This is important t' me, Cassie. I'll never rest till I remember. But I won't leave you, no matter what."

He wasn't sure he really meant it.

She looked up at him with sorrowful eyes. "Promise?"

He wasn't really sure of anything.

"I promise."

"What the devil is goin' on out here?"

Homer Lonnegan came around the corner with his Navy Colt drawn and ready.

Red Bear nodded. "Hello, Mr. Lonnegan."

"Red Bear! I hope you have some more honey to sell."

Raider shook his head. "Red Bear an' me have some work t' do."

Lonnegan hesitated. "Oh—You gonna be back in time to help me in the mine today?"

"I hope so," the big man replied. "I sure as hell hope so."

Raider was surprised at the energy possessed by the old man. Red Bear preceded him up the trail, climbing as quickly as a scared ground squirrel. Raider had to stop for a couple of minutes at one point because his head was spinning. He wondered if his noggin would ever be the same. Hadn't he once been a Pinkerton agent, a man that others depended on? Now he was just a miner, answering to Mr. Lonnegan and his future bride.

"Catch me if you can," Red Bear called from above.

His memory jogged again. He seemed to recall chasing Red Bear before. Or was it someone else?

"Hurry up, cowboy," the Indian called again.

Cowboy. He hated being called that. Had he once been a wrangler? If he had, he had hated that too. His head was spinning faster. What the hell was happening inside his skull?

"Come on, Pinkerton. It's right up here."

Raider staggered up the rocky path. Sweat dripped from

every pore in his body. What the hell did Red Bear have waiting for him up there? He heard the voice, only it was a long way off.

Lawman. Look out!

"It's right here, big man."

He stumbled onto the ledge, holding the Colt in front of him. "Where?" he asked. "Where is it?"

Red Bear pointed to the ground. "Right here was where it happened. Don't you remember? You chased me and you ended up here."

His eyes would not focus. Aching in his skull. What the hell had happened? Why couldn't he remember?

"They were in the trees," Red Bear went on. "They shot at you. I yelled. The bullet still caught you. You fell off right here."

He took Raider's arm and led him to the edge of the cliff. The big man looked down into the blue pool of water. He stumbled again, almost falling headlong for the second time.

Why wouldn't it come to him?

"Don't you remember, Raider? Can't you see it? You looked up into the trees. What did you see?"

"I don't know, damn it!"

Red Bear exhaled impatiently. "I didn't want to have to do it, but I can see it's the only way."

"I cain't see it," Raider said, his head still reeling. "It ain't clear."

"It will be," the Indian replied. "It will be."

Red Bear led him up into the trees. "Stay right there."

Raider felt sick at his stomach. He leaned back and watched as the Shoshone picked up a small shovel. The Indian began to dig in the soft earth. Raider screamed when the smell reached his nostrils.

"Dead men," he cried. "Dead men."

Red Bear pointed at him. "Five of them. Four Pinkertons, like you, and a sheriff from Boise. Do I have to show you the bodies?"

"Stanton," the big man said. "I remember. His hand—his suit. He didn't have no face."

"You've got to stop them," Red Bear said. "You've got to—"

But Raider was off and running down the slope. The Indian followed his long strides. Raider stopped when he reached the bottom of the treeline. He was back in the clearing. Sweat poured off his face.

"Do you see it?" the Indian cried.

"Idaho! I'm in Idaho. Wagner sent me!"

"Yes, yes!"

Raider pointed to the south. "The mine—Morgan, not Lonnegan. I was at Morgan's. Working. I went up on a rope. Almost fell down."

"More!"

The big man touched his forehead. "Why was I here? Galler! I saw Galler. And the man was killed in Boise. I don't remember his name. Sheriff locked me up. Had to send a wire to Wagner."

"Don't stop, Pinkerton! Not now!"

It was all spinning around, like an eddy in a swollen river. Murky and deep, a stream with no bottom. A raging current that wanted to sweep him away into the white rapids.

Raider had to struggle to keep his balance. "It's fuzzy, Red Bear."

The Shoshone helped to steady him. "Here, drink this." He brought a clay flask out of his pocket.

Raider drank the hot, dark liquid. Indian brew. It hit his stomach like a keg of coal oil. He swallowed what he could and then spat out the rest.

"Don't stop," Red Bear said. "Don't quit on me."

Raider tried to shake off the dizziness. "Galler. I went to see him. Then he was gone. I came up here."

"You're on the path, white man."

The trail. He was on the trail. Coming north. Stop in McCall. On to Cascade. No. The signs on the road. "Morgan!"

Red Bear nodded. "You're gettin' closer."

"Morgan painted over Galler's sign," Raider said. "He took the mine from Galler. Kidnapped Galler."

"Keep it goin'."

His head grew black inside.

"I cain't remember no more, Red Bear."

"Damn it, man, you have to. Before it's too late. You followed me up here, after you worked for Morgan in the mine."

A streak of pain shot through his skull, but with it came more images. "Couldn't catch you,' he said. "Too fast. On that damned burrow. Led me in circles. Came here."

"What did you see?"

"The dead body of Stanton."

Red Bear grabbed his shoulders and shook him. "After that? What did you see after that?"

Raider pushed him away. "Nothin'. I didn't see nothin'. I went t' the edge o' the cliff. I looked down at my horse. It was still there. But that's all I remember."

"No, you looked up into the trees."

Raider wheeled suddenly, staring back into the forest. "They were comin' down at me."

"Who?"

"Both of 'em." He looked at the Indian. "The shawmee. The one that comes t' claim his bride. He was with her. The girl. But I knew her. An' I saw her after that."

"Where? Where did you see her?"

His black eyes were glazed over. "In Cascade. She looked out of a window at me. Only I couldn't remember her then."

"Who was she?"

His forehead ached. Lowering his eyes. Where had he seen the girl?

"You had her picture in your saddlebag!" Red Bear cried.

Raider's head jerked up. He stared into the trees as it all came back. Why hadn't he remembered before?

"The Galler girl," he said. "She was with the big Indian. And he was the one at Morgan's mine. The one who pulled me up the rope."

Red Bear whooped and began a little war dance.

Raider laughed, slowly at first and then like a madman. "Morgan is usin' the girl. That's how he got all the others. Just like me. They froze when they saw her with the Indian. He's makin' her pretend that she's the lost bride, the one that the spirit takes in the spring."

He saw her again, gliding down through the trees in her white, flowing gown. Her hair was long and reddish, just like her father's. He remembered freezing, like a rabbit under a jacklight. He didn't want to hurt the girl. And the Indian wasn't armed.

Then he heard Red Bear shouting his warning.

A rifle went off.
Staggering.
Falling.
Darkness.
He heard the shot again.
Red Bear turned to the south. "Did you hear that?"
There really had been a shot. It echoed through the mountains. Another burst came right behind it.
"My God," Raider said. "It's comin' from Lonnegan's place."
They started down the path, heading for the gunshots that resounded through the morning, making the big man fear what he might find when he reached the Lonnegan mine.

Raider jumped into the chestnut's saddle, galloping straight up the creek bed for the cabin. Red Bear was behind him although the stallion left the burro in a hurry. Raider came around the bend to see the four riders circling the house, firing shots into the windows.
"Hyah!"
His spurs urged the chestnut into the battle. Raider brought up the Winchester, cranking a shell into the chamber. The four men on horseback didn't see him until the first round knocked one of them out of the saddle.
Raider levered the rifle again.
The riders reined their mounts.
A second round from the rifle dropped another one. He fell to the earth, clutching his chest. The others didn't even bother to help their dying cohort. They rode quickly in the other direction, following the downstream flow of the creek.
The big man cut them off. He turned his horse to the left, biting a straighter path to the back entrance of the ravine. The men aimed at him and made the mistake of firing. Until that point, Raider had planned to take them alive. Their shots only made him angry.
He fired twice, one bullet for each man.
They both fell. He wondered if all four were dead. He shouldn't have lost his temper. Then he thought: Hell, boy, that's how you kept from getting killed all these years.
He slowed the stallion and climbed down to look at his handiwork.

Two clean shots through the chest.

"These boys ain't gonna talk."

He started back on foot, to see if the other two were gone. His heart was pounding.

He looked for Cassie and Homer, hoping they would come running out of the house. He called to them. Nothing.

Check the bodies first. Procedure. Wagner always said that a Pinkerton should follow procedure.

To hell with procedure, he thought.

His foot splintered the door of the cabin.

Cassie looked up at him, tears in her blue eyes. Homer Lonnegan's head lay in her lap. Blood oozed from the bullet wound in his gut.

"He tried to stand up to them," Cassie said weakly. "But there were too many of them."

"Not anymore," the big man replied coldly. "Is he dead?"

Her face turned hateful. "You! You Pinkerton bastard! It's all your fault. They came here to kill you!"

The words cut him as deeply as any he had ever heard. But he had to stay tough. The Pinkerton in him knew there was work to do.

"Damn it, Cassie, is he alive?"

She nodded.

Raider bent down to look at the wound. It was on the right side of Lonnegan's stomach. The old boy still had breath left in him.

Lonnegan stirred and opened his eyes. "Gut shot, Blackie. It ain't no way for a man to die."

"You ain't gonna die, Homer."

Tears welled in his eyes and he began to cry like a baby. "It burns, Blackie. It burns bad."

"I know, Homer. I been shot a bunch myself."

Cassie's expression had grown more hopeful. "Can you help him?"

Raider grimaced and exhaled. "I don't know. I seen worse. If it didn't hit anything important, he might just make it."

He stood up.

Cassie glared at him. "Where you goin'?"

"T' get the Injun."

"Why?"

He started for the door. "Because Injuns know 'bout medicine an' stuff. Just keep him warm. And boil some water."

Red Bear was standing over the first two men that Raider had killed.

"Tie up that burro," the big man said. "We gotta save ol' Lonnegan. You got any more of that Injun brew?"

Red Bear nodded and then pointed to the bodies. "Haskell brothers. Cousins to the Pilots. They wanted revenge because you killed Esky."

"I reckon they didn't get it, did they?"

The Indian shrugged. "Guess not."

"If you know so much," Raider challenged, "then why don't you go in there an' help ol' Lonnegan. He's been gut shot. See if you can get the bullet out."

"We'll do it together," Red Bear said.

"You don't seem too upset by all this."

The same shrug. "It's hard to get riled about the doin's of white men. You're all so crazy."

Raider wasn't going to argue the point.

Inside, Red Bear rolled Lonnegan on his good side. "Won't have to get the bullet out," he said to Raider. "Went right through him. See. Came out right here."

Cassie turned away, gagging.

Raider went to her and put his hand on her shoulder. "He's gonna be all right, Cassie."

She looked up at him, her eyes filled with tears. "Raider, I'm sorry about what I said. You—I—"

He hugged her. Cassie sobbed on his chest, putting her arms around him. Another man had promised to marry her. Not the big Pinkerton who had regained his memory.

Red Bear shook his head, groaning. "If you two could stop long enough to find me the things I need—"

Cassie peered hopefully toward the old Shoshone. "I'll get you anything you want, Red Bear."

"A big sewing needle," he said. "Some hair from the tail of a horse. Hot water and whiskey. That should do it."

Cassie hurried to accommodate him.

Raider squinted skeptically at the old shaman. "Whiskey? What d' you need whiskey for?"

"To clean the wound. And to have a drink."

The big man could not argue with that.

In less than an hour, they had Homer Lonnegan safely in

bed, his wound stitched and cleaned. "Wouldn't mind havin' a slug of that corn liquor myself," the old boy said as they lowered him onto the sheets.

"Not with a gut wound," Red Bear said. "Don't give him any water until tomorrow. If he gets dry, wet his lips with a cloth. And don't you move, Mr. Lonnegan. Stay as still as you can."

The old man nodded and closed his eyes.

Cassie sat down beside the bed. She had a bowl of water and a cloth. Her gentle hands dabbed at his forehead.

"I think he's goin' to live," Red Bear said with wry certainty. "I've always known the white man to be tough. He's like lice; sometimes you just can't get rid of him."

Raider grabbed the old shaman by the scruff of the neck. "Come on, Cochise, you're gonna help me get rid of at least one white man."

"Cochise was Apache," the Shoshone replied. "Apaches are dogs. They drink horse piss and—"

Raider dragged him outside, where they could talk.

"You don't have to be rough," Red Bear said. "We're partners now."

Raider scowled at the wrinkled, smiling brown face. "Any partner of mine don't stay alive very long."

"I'll take that chance. Besides, it will take more than a white man to kill me."

"Morgan?" Raider said.

Red Bear nodded. "It's about time he got his."

A cool breeze had begun to blow through the ravine.

Raider's face slacked into a grin. "Thanks for savin' the old man."

"Ah. It wasn't much. He probably would have lived anyway."

Raider hunkered down, staring in the direction of the mine. He was quiet for a long time before he told Red Bear to go in and get the whiskey. They drank it slowly, chasing it with water to cool the burn.

Finally the big man turned to the Shoshone and said: "I think I done figgered it, Red Bear. But you're gonna have t' help."

"Like I said before, just leave somethin' for me."

He turned to look at the rough-hewn Pinkerton, only to be

startled by the strange, glassy glow in Raider's black eyes. Never had he seen that kind of fire in a white man. Never.

"We're gonna kick Morgan's ass," the big man offered. "We're gonna kick it good. I got it all planned."

Using his finger as a stylus, he began to draw a diagram in the dirt. It wasn't a difficult ploy, especially when he compared it with some of the things he had pulled off in the past. But the old feeling had returned, the thrill of the hunt, the manipulation of unknown factors. This was why he had become a Pinkerton in the first place.

It felt good to remember. It felt good to know things.

Raider was back.

CHAPTER EIGHTEEN

Raider waited in the first cool breezes of early evening, crouched behind a boulder near the ledge where he had been tricked the first time. The plan had been set in motion. Red Bear had to come through for it to work. The big man wondered if he could trust the old Shoshone, even though it was a little late to be worrying about it.

Something moved in the trees above the ledge. Raider raised up, peeking over the boulder. A big buck mule deer and three does moved gingerly through the forest. He let out a deep breath. No Indian yet. No girl.

The girl was the key, he thought. Morgan had kidnapped Cynthia Galler so he could use her to trick anyone who came into the hills to look for him. Surely Morgan knew about the legend of the shawmee, the Indian spirit who supposedly came every spring to claim his bride.

The big man shook off the chill that ran along his shoulders. Morgan had to be one sick son of a bitch to use an innocent girl like that. But hadn't the plan been perfect? Hadn't Raider bit on the ruse when he saw her coming down the mountain, flanked by that Shoshone who worked for Morgan? Stanton had bit too. And they had both been bitten by the same rifle. The outcome had been a little better for Raider.

"You're one lucky son of a gun," he said to himself.

The sun was getting lower. He had to wonder if Morgan was going to come after him. No doubt the dapper thief had sent the four cousins of Esky Pilot to do his dirty work for him. Only they had failed, thanks to the Winchester in Raider's scabbard.

The rifle lay next to him, leaning against the boulder. Shined and ready. He'd have to be careful though. No need to shoot the girl.

He tried to remember the picture of Cynthia Galler. Was it really her that he saw looking out the window in Cascade? Probably not. Morgan probably had her stashed in some dark barn, trotting her out for the deception. The girl in the window had been someone else, someone who looked like her.

Raider still wasn't sure how a weakling like Morgan had masterminded the plan. He didn't seem to be anything more than a dandy, a man in a suit who gave orders to others. That was the key—give the orders and let others carry them out. It didn't matter who you were or how strong you were, as long as you could hire your own muscle.

Wasn't it the same with Raider and his bosses? Pinkerton and Wagner hired him to do their dirty work. No, it wasn't the same. Raider stayed on the right side of the law, at least most of the time.

Another sound in the forest. The mule deer were still feeding. Maybe Morgan and crew wouldn't come. Maybe they'd smell the trap. Although Raider didn't see how he could have figured it any better. As plans went, it seemed fine. Of course, nothing ever went exactly the way you figured it, even when the plan worked.

He looked over the edge of the boulder again. Where were they? Maybe Red Bear had chickened out. After all, Morgan probably wasn't too happy about the Indian helping Raider the first time.

But this was different. Red Bear was supposed to slink into Morgan's camp, acting hangdog and repent. He was supposed to tell Morgan that he was sorry that he helped Raider. Tell him the big Pinkerton planned to return to the mountains to look for the bodies of his associates. Tell him Raider believed the story about the shawmee, say he hoped to see the spirit again, to ask it for directions. That would probably be enough to draw Morgan out again. If he bought it.

Raider leaned back against the boulder. He wondered if they would come up the same trail he had taken. Maybe they had another path into the trees. If Morgan wasn't tough, he was at least smart. Look at the way he had taken the Galler girl and her father.

The big man remembered Galler's den, how it looked after the mining man had been taken. No sign of a struggle. While somebody was killing Galler's associate (Hadn't Burden been his name?) another man, maybe Morgan himself, was talking to Galler, telling him that he had better come peacefully or his daughter would be killed.

Raider's brow fretted and he exhaled. Why would Morgan have waited so long to confront Galler about his daughter? Morgan could have played his hand at any time, but he delayed almost two months. No doubt Galler himself was the final card in the hand, the fifth spade to the flush, the ace to the high straight. Raider figured to ask Morgan personally, after he was caught.

Another noise stirred the quiet of the forest.

Raider looked up to see the mule deer spooking, running away from the sound. Somebody up there. Red Bear? Or had Morgan taken the bait?

The big man figured he had to show himself to get things started.

Rising, he slipped out from behind the boulder, striding toward the trees. Did he hear voices whispering like the wind? Keep steady. Try to make enough noise so they would hear him. Make sure he didn't let the rifle bite him a second time.

"Hey," he called. "Anybody there?"

Nothing.

He searched the shadows above him. Almost dark. Suddenly it seemed like a stupid plan. Best just to turn, get down the hill, head back to Boise to get the sheriff, or maybe wait for the marshal in Cascade.

But the time had come to finish it.

He heard the rustling in the trees. A white shape fluttered like the backside of a mule deer. Only it wasn't a deer. It was the flowing cloth of a white dress.

Cynthia Galler was dressed like a bride. Flowers in her red

hair. Beside her walked the big Indian. Raider had to give it to Morgan; he had come up with a wild plan. So wild that it had worked on five Pinkertons and a sheriff.

The Galler girl made strange vocal sounds.

The Indian grunted.

Morgan had coached them well. Probably threatened the girl by saying he would kill her father if she didn't go along with it. What a sneaky bastard. He had to be hiding somewhere in the woods, taking a bead on Raider with his rifle. The big man looked away from the girl and the Indian, scanning the forest for the glint of rifle steel. Would there be enough light in the dusk?

"Come on down, Morgan," he called to the trees. "It's over."

Hesitation in the woods. The girl and the Indian froze in the trees. Rifle lever chortling, echoing in the dusk. Raider anticipated the burst from the weapon. He lunged forward, hitting the ground as the rifle went off. Muzzle flashing in the shadows.

Raider aimed for the flash and fired twice.

"Get him," Morgan called from his hiding place. "Kill him you red-skinned bastard!"

The Indian gave a whooping war cry. Raider looked up to see him charging forward, a knife in his thick hand. The first shot from the Winchester hit him in the chest. The Indian stopped, looking at the bullet hole as if he could not believe that he had been shot.

Raider fired again. The second slug knocked the Shoshone to the ground. He lay there screeching, writhing in agony for the last few moments of his life. Raider levered the Winchester, expecting another burst from Morgan.

"Help me!" the girl cried. "Help me!"

He had to go get her, even if it meant that Morgan might draw a bead on him. Rising, he ran headlong up the incline, digging toward the young woman in the white dress. Morgan's rifle barked again. Raider stopped and returned fire. That seemed to quiet the other gun.

Cynthia Galler was trembling when he reached her.

"Get down, girl. You wanna have your fool head shot off?"

She wrapped her arms around him, clinging tightly. "Thank God! Thank God you saved me!"

"Easy, honey. I gotta go find the man that did this to you."

"No!" she screamed. "Don't leave me. Please—oh God, please don't leave me."

She seemed so pitiful that Raider had to stay with her. He looked back into the trees, wondering if Morgan was going to fire again. The dandified claim jumper was a lousy shot. Raider waited, hoping he'd get another muzzle flash to aim at.

But Morgan didn't fire again. Sounds of someone running away. He probably had a horse back there. A couple of them if he had brought the girl and the Indian.

He started to get up, to go after him.

"No," the girl cried. "Stay with me. Don't let them take me again."

Raider exhaled. She was so pale and fragile-looking. She might not last in the mountains if he left her to fend for herself.

"Okay, honey. I ain't goin' nowhere."

She clung tightly to him, pressing her face into his arm.

Raider turned her face up so he could see her. "Honey, that man, Morgan. Can you take me to him? You know where he is?"

She nodded.

"Where is he?"

"Cascade," she said weakly.

"Is your paw there too?"

She nodded.

Raider urged her to her feet. "Time t' ride. Let's go settle accounts with that bast—with Morgan."

She seemed more than eager to come along with him.

Raider found Morgan's other two horses hidden in the trees. He mounted up on a black stallion. The girl wanted to ride behind him. He figured it was best. The animal looked strong enough to carry tandem.

"Hold on tight," he told her.

She nodded, wrapping her arms around his waist.

Raider urged the black down a narrow path. The trail led out of the trees, onto a high ridge. He could see the first lights of Cascade in the distance, a faint glow on the horizon. Morgan didn't have much of a head start, so he might not be hard to catch.

The big man figured to be wary of him, until he had the ropes around his wrists. Morgan had been keen in the execution of his spook show. Had even left himself a way to escape. He knew Raider would stay with the girl if things went wrong.

Even in the darkness, the black made good time. Raider didn't remember much about the trail, but the animal seemed to know it. Sure it did. Morgan had made the trip to the mountain at least six times. He had taken the four missing Pinkertons and the sheriff to their reward.

How was he going to tell Wagner that they were all dead?

Best to worry about that after he had captured Morgan. Keep on top of it. Don't end up like his associates.

He slowed the black when he neared Cascade. His approach was cautious. He slid up behind the first building he reached on the edge of town. Dismounting, he pulled the girl down beside him.

"What are we doing?" she asked softly.

Raider touched her shoulder. She looked so pretty in the white dress. Red and yellow flowers in her hair. She could have passed for the beautiful bride of a rich man. Cassie Lonnegan went in and out of his thoughts.

"My father," she said. "Help him."

Raider put a finger to his lips. "Easy now. You gotta show me where Morgan has your paw. Can you remember?"

She nodded. "I think so."

"Okay, let's go. Slow-like. An' if I tell you to stay put, you stay put. Understand?"

She nodded again, frowning pitifully. Morgan had cut her deep. The big man aimed to see that he paid for it.

They started down the dark street.

Laughter erupted from a porch in front of the general store.

Raider counted four men sitting on kegs and in wooden chairs.

As they passed, one of the men tipped his hat. "Evenin', Miss Galler. Is that you, Mr. Morgan?"

Raider hesitated, thinking that Morgan must have paraded the young woman all over Cascade. Just couldn't resist showing what a ladies' man he was. Raider tipped his hat to the man.

One of the other men said, "Hey, that ain't Morgan."

Cynthia Galler turned back to the man. "This is my uncle,"

she said quickly. "Came all the way from Boise."

Raider hurried her along. "Good goin', Cindy."

She clung tightly to his arm. "We're almost there. You've got to save my father, Mr. Raider."

"I will, honey. I promise."

They stopped across the street from a brown building that looked familiar to Raider. He saw the curtained window where he had seen the face of the young woman who now stood at his side. It had been Cynthia Galler. Morgan had been keeping her in Cascade.

She pointed to the window. "There."

Raider saw that the casement was dark.

"Is your father there?" he asked.

She nodded.

Maybe Morgan was sitting in there without a light. He asked the girl if there was an easy way up to the second floor of the building. She replied that the stairs were in the back.

Raider exhaled. He didn't want to stomp around in the dark. He wanted to see what he was shooting at. If Robert Galler was going to stay alive, better that he didn't catch a stray bullet in the shadows.

"Where else might Morgan be?" he asked.

Cynthia Galler lowered her eyes. "I don't know."

"Shit!"

"What?"

He patted her back. "Nothin', honey. I was just—"

A gaslight glowed to life in the window across the street. Raider could see shadows behind the lace curtains where he had seen the girl before. Morgan had made it home. Raider wondered if he would run or fight.

"Are those stairs the only way in?"

The girl nodded.

"I could get on the roof. Mebbe swing down through the window."

"Hurry," she said. "Before he gets away."

"He ain't gonna run, honey."

"No?"

Raider shook his head and smiled. "A pack rat don't leave its nest, not unless you burn him out."

She leaned back against the wall of the alleyway where they had been hiding. "Don't make me go in there."

Raider squinted at her. "He did things to you. Didn't he?"
She nodded, looking away like she was ashamed.
Raider grimaced. "I'll try t' keep from killin' him," he told her. "Let him live t' face the noose. He seems like the kind who'll cry a lot afore they drop the gallows door."
"I hope so," she said, her face contorting into a hateful expression. "I hope he burns in hell."
"He will, honey. He prob'ly will."

Raider took the girl by the shoulders and turned her to him. "Honey, I want you t' go t' the sheriff's office. Tell him what I'm doin'. Tell him t' meet me across the street. Can you do that?"
She nodded. Raider wasn't sure he felt comfortable about entrusting her to carry the message to the sheriff. But he had no choice. Morgan might hurt Robert Galler. Best to get it over quick.
"Has he got any guns in there?"
"I don't know," the girl replied. "He never showed any guns to me."
"Not even when he kidnapped you?"
Her face slacked and she started to cry.
"Easy, girl. Now you wait until I get across the street an' then you go for the sheriff. You know where his office is?"
She nodded again.
"If he don't know me, tell him I'm the man who killed Esky Pilot. You got that? Esky Pilot."
She mouthed the name.
Raider thought Cynthia Galler looked to be at the end of her rope. "Are you sure you can make it?"
She said she could.
Raider kissed her softly on the cheek, a brotherly peck. "I'm gonna go get your paw, darlin'. Ever'thin' is gonna be all right."
A weak smile crossed her thin lips.
Raider turned and stomped toward the brown building. He could hear music and laughter from the saloon. Was it Saturday night? Maybe he'd have a snort after the sheriff locked up Morgan.
He slipped into the alley that led to the stairs.
Stopping, leaning against the wall, he drew the Colt and

thumbed the hammer. He listened, but the music was too loud. He didn't hear a thing from upstairs. Morgan probably wasn't so tough without his rifle and the big Indian to back him up.

Slowly Raider started down the alleyway, inching along with his back to the wall. Still no sound from above. He hoped Galler was safe.

Mr. Raider. It came out of nowhere. A flash.

Cynthia had called him by name. Why did the thought strike him just now? He hadn't told her his name. He shook it off. Morgan had probably been complaining about Raider around the girl.

His head spun a little. Some of the dizziness came back. No time for this, he told himself. Settle down. Keep going.

When he rounded the corner, he saw the stairs in front of him.

The door opened above. Raider slid back into a shadow. Hardy Morgan came out and threw something over the railing. Water splashed against the building across the alleyway. Morgan went back inside.

Sweat poured down Raider's rugged face. He wiped his forehead with the back of his arm. Should have taken him right then, but the shot wasn't clear. The railing of the stairs had been in the way.

He looked down at his gun hand. He was trembling. A weakness spread through his body. Not now, he told himself. Not now.

He wasn't afraid. It was the wound on his head. He had been going strong and now he was almost out of breath.

His stomach turned a little. He thought about the girl, about what Morgan had probably done to her. Get the bastard. Make him pay.

His legs were wobbly as he started for the stairs.

First step. What the hell was happening to him? He steadied himself against the railing. His lips were dry.

A rain barrel rested next to the stairs, under a drain pipe. Raider staggered over to the barrel and plunged his head into the cold water. He drank deep, hoping it would help.

When he pulled his head out, he felt better. It still wasn't like him to be nervous before he took a man, not like this.

That damned wound on his head was still acting like a raw bronc at breaking time.

"To hell with it," he said to himself.

He turned away from the barrel and started up the stairs.

His vision had blurred some but he could see well enough to find the door. He heard Morgan inside, stomping around. Probably not too happy about Raider foiling his plot on the mountain. Raider wanted to smile but he was still dizzy.

Damn his head.

Morgan said something to another man.

Galler was in there.

Raider leaned around, peering into a window. He could see the older man tied to a chair. A gag kept him from speaking. He also got his first glimpse of Morgan, who did not seem to be carrying a gun.

He looked back over his shoulder, wondering if the girl had gotten to the sheriff yet.

Hell, when had he ever depended on a lawman?

Stepping back, he leaned against the railing to brace himself. He took a deep breath, feeling all the strength that was left in his legs. One good kick. That's all he needed.

The door flew open when he applied his Justin boot.

Pain in his foot.

Head still spinning.

Sweat burning his eyes.

He saw Morgan scurrying for a cubbyhole in a desk.

Raider stepped in, lifting the Colt in front of him.

Morgan started to turn with a small pocket revolver in hand.

The big man waved him off. "No you don't, Morgan. Not unless you want to be suckin' air through a hole in your chest."

The dapper gentleman seemed to wilt. His whole body was shaking. Raider knew not to let up, even if his head was aching. A cornered cougar trembled like a willow leaf, but it could still tear your throat out.

"Get rid o' the gun," he told Morgan.

"I—you don't understand—"

"No, I don't. That man Burden was killed with a pistol like the one you're holdin'."

Raider started across the room, watching Morgan in the

light from the gas lamp. Without taking his eyes off the revolver, he patted Robert Galler on the shoulder. He told the old man it was going to be all right, that he would untie him as soon as Morgan dropped the gun.

Raising the Colt, he said: "I mean it, boy. Don't make me shoot you. Throw the gun over there by the door."

Morgan seemed to be frozen by his fear.

"Damn it, Morgan, do like I say!"

His face had turned white. Sweat seeped through his coat. Spittle flowed from his lips.

"The sheriff's on his way," the big man offered.

Morgan glanced at the door.

"Yeah, that's right. He's comin'. Now just chuck that gun over by the door and I'll see to it that you get a nice, tight noose."

Morgan fumbled with the weapon, finally managing to throw it toward the threshold. The revolver hit and slid onto the landing outside. Morgan leaned back against the desk, gripping the sides for balance.

Raider waved the barrel of the Colt again. "Hands to the sky."

Morgan started to cry. Raider couldn't believe it. He whimpered like a little girl. The big man still didn't trust him.

"I said put those hands up."

"I'll fall."

Raider took one hostile step toward the quivering lawbreaker.

Morgan put up his hands immediately.

Raider smiled at him. "You ain't so big without your rifle."

He reached over to untie Galler. His body had settled down some, even if his head continued to hurt. Best not to forget that Morgan was the one who gave him the wound in the first place.

When he looked back at the dapper bandit, Morgan had started to move slowly toward the door.

"I'll drop you if you move another inch," the big man said.

Morgan stuttered, slobber rolling off his tongue. "You don't understand. It's not like you think."

"I think you shot me," Raider replied. "You also shot four o' my buddies and a sheriff. Not t' mention kidnappin' this boy an' his daughter."

Galler had wriggled out of his loosened bonds. He took off the gag that Morgan had tied around his head. "Thank you, Raider."

"Don't sweat it, honcho."

"My daughter," Galler said in a tired voice. "Where is she?"

"Sent her for the sheriff," the big man replied.

Galler's eyes widened. "What?"

"I sent her for the sheriff," he repeated. "In fact, I think I hear 'em comin' up the stairs."

"No," Galler cried. "You don't understand—"

The old man stood, only to fall to the floor.

Raider bent over him. "You all right?"

"Cynthia—she's—"

"She's right here, daddy!"

Cynthia Galler came into the room holding the pocket revolver.

"Good," Raider said. "Where's the sheriff?"

"He's been delayed," the girl said in a clear voice.

Her eyes were wide. A steady hand gripped the small pistol. Raider was afraid she might shoot Morgan.

"Let me have the gun, honey," he said. "You can take care o' your paw. He's—"

Cynthia Galler turned and pointed the gun at Raider. "You're the one who's going to drop his gun."

Raider hesitated. His Colt was pointed at the floor. What the hell did she think she was doing?

"Look here, girl—"

"Drop it," she said. "Or you get it right between the eyes."

CHAPTER NINETEEN

Hardy Morgan took a step toward Cynthia Galler. "Do as she says, Pinkerton. She will shoot you without hesitation."

Raider grimaced. The damned woman had the drop on him. He could raise the Colt and kill her, but she would probably get off a shot and put a bullet in his chest. What the hell was going on?

"Drop it," she insisted. "I'm not playing with you, Raider."

He let his gun fall to the floor. "I knew," he said. "You called me by name. You covered too quick with those men at the general store. You came along with me without a hitch."

"I was acting," she said proudly.

Morgan bent and gave her a kiss on the cheek. "You didn't let me down."

She grinned from ear to ear. "Have I ever?"

Raider gestured to her father, who was lying on the floor. "What about him? He don't look too good."

Cynthia Galler shrugged. "He'll live. And if he doesn't, who cares?"

"He's your pappy!" the big man replied.

She frowned. "Get his gun, Hardy."

Morgan obeyed her without hesitation. He picked up

Raider's Colt and hefted it, thumbing back the hammer. "So," he said with a triumphant leer, "the tables seemed to have turned."

Raider scowled at the weak-faced dandy. "Gotta hand it to you, Morgan. Never figgered you were the kind t' pull off somethin' like this."

Cynthia Galler cackled like a witch. "Are you crazy?" she said. "None of this was Hardy's idea. I came up with it all by myself."

"Why'd you kill Burden?" Raider asked quickly.

The thin line of the girl's mouth tightened into a smirk. "He was dangerous. He wanted too much."

"Then he was in on the plan?"

She nodded. "For a while. He brought in Hardy. Called him Hunt Kreeger." She smiled at Morgan. "But we soon took care of that, didn't we, honey?"

Morgan smiled back. "Yes, dear."

"We had to kill him, you see," the redheaded girl went on. "He was asking too much. He wanted control over the old man there."

Raider glanced at Robert Galler, who still lay on the floor. "Let me help him back into the chair."

As he started to move toward Galler, Cynthia waved him away with the pocket revolver. "Don't. Let him lie. He's nothing to me."

"He's your father!" the big man cried. "How can you go agin him? How can you treat him like this?"

She took a few steps toward the window, glaring all the time at the old gentleman on the floor. "Father? He's not my real father. He married my mother a couple of years ago, after his first wife died. I was never a daughter to him."

Raider wasn't sure he believed her. "He never told me that. He said he loved you. That he was lost without you."

Her lips tightened into an even more hateful expression. "Lost? Did he really say that? Yes, he was lost. I left his bed. You see, after my mother died, he expected me to fulfill her wifely duties. He couldn't stand it when I went to another man. I love Hardy, not him."

Something clicked in Raider's head. The small footprints in Galler's house, after he had disappeared. "You," he said to the girl, "you came to see Galler while Hardy was killin'

Burden. That's why he went with you, didn't put up a fight."

"You're good," the girl replied. "Much better than the four who came before you."

"So let me see if I got this straight," he went on. "The original plan called for Morgan an' Burden to' d'liver bogus reports t' your—t' Mr. Galler. Tell him the mines up north were dry. Convince him that his company was goin' bust."

"He is good," said Hardy Morgan.

"Lucky too," the girl rejoined.

"What were you gonna do?" Raider asked. "Bring in somebody else t' buy the mine out from under him? Pay nothin'."

Morgan shrugged. "It doesn't sound so bad when you put it like that. Just business."

Raider shook his head disgustedly. "Business, huh? Cheatin' a man after he's worked all his life for somethin'. Stabbin' him in the back after he took you into his confidence."

"Moralize all you want," Cynthia Galler replied. "It's not going to save your life."

"Gonna kill me right now?" he asked.

She shook her head, grinning. "Oh no. Yours will be a slow death. We have plans for you."

"Which one of you killed Burden? Was it you, Hardy?"

"No," Morgan replied.

The girl chortled derisively. "Hardy would never have the guts to pull off something like that. No, it was the Shoshone. The one you killed in the mountains. He pulled the trigger on Burden."

Raider thought about Red Bear. "What about the other Indian? The ol' man who told you 'bout me."

"He's dead," the girl replied. "Don't worry about him. He's resting in the happy hunting ground."

Raider felt a twinge of guilt. He had sent Red Bear straight into the fire. The old man's luck had finally run out.

"Funny," Morgan said. "Red Bear only came around right before you arrived, Pinkerton. I wonder why he didn't help the others?"

"No matter," the girl offered. "We have to get these two locked up. I don't want them running around loose. Hardy, why don't you tie up the old man? And then this big one."

"I don't have any rope, Cynthia."

She sighed, the way a mother sighs when she's become

impatient with a child. "Honestly, Hardy, do I have to do everything myself? Use the rope on the floor, the one that the old boy was tied with before."

Hardy moved to retie Galler to the chair.

Raider wanted to keep them talking. Wait for the chance. Surely he could move against the girl and Morgan. Even if they did have the guns, Raider felt he could take them. Just wait for the right moment.

"The spook show," he continued. "That your idea, Hardy? Or did little missie here come up with that one?"

Cynthia straightened proudly. "I thought of that. I heard the legend all over this territory. How romantic. An Indian spirit who returns for his bride. It was easy to stage. I thought of it when I saw that the first Pinkerton agent was not going to give up until he found me."

"We're like that," Raider offered.

"Yes, but what good does it do you? You're only going to end up dead. And you won't be as lucky as your friends. You're going to die a lot slower. You'll pray for death before we're finished with you."

Raider glanced sideways at her. "You know, Cindy, you're right lippy. Cain't say as I like that in a woman."

She sneered back at him. "Slap him, Hardy. "

Morgan looked skeptical. "Cynthia, I don't think—"

"Ooh, you weakling!" She started forward but then looked as if she had second thoughts. "You're right, Hardy. We'll get him later."

Raider wanted her to come closer. He wanted to grab that revolver from her hand and slap the shit out of her. But she was too smart, like a baby cougar playing with a rattler, staying just out of range of the strike.

"Hurry up," she said to Morgan.

The white-faced dandy had finished tying Galler to the chair. The old man had lost consciousness. Raider wondered if he would live.

Morgan eyed the big man cautiously. "I'm out of rope, Cindy. What should I do?"

"Go get some, you fool. I'll watch him. Give me that gun."

Morgan handed her the Colt and then started down the stairs.

Cynthia Galler shook her head. "That idiot. If he weren't so handsome, I'd have gotten rid of him long ago."

"Cain't really say as I care for your disposition," Raider said. "You're right ornery for a girl."

"Just watching out for myself," she replied. "Nobody else is going to do it for me."

Raider gestured toward a couch on the other side of the room. "Mind if I sit down?"

She raised both weapons at him. "Don't move."

He wondered if the knife in his boot might do him some good. He would be able to reach it if he sat down. But he had to be cagey. The redheaded outlaw was as tough as any man he had fought against. Maybe not as strong, but certainly just as wily.

"You know, Cindy, you're a mighty pretty young woman. It's a shame you're stuck with a weakling like Hardy. Mebbe you could use a man who was stronger. A man who could take care o' you."

She laughed. "A man like you?"

Raider shrugged. "You could do worse. And I'd druther join you than fight you. How 'bout it?"

"What about the Lonnegan girl?"

The big man's face slacked into a frown. "Leave her outta this. She ain't got nothin' t' do with you."

Cynthia Galler showed him her hateful smirk. "Just as I thought. You're in love with that little wallflower."

"Leave her alone!"

"I'll stomp her!" the girl cried. "I'll crush her like a June bug if she gets in my way."

"Like you crushed your paw?"

"I told you, he's not my real father. My real father was a riverboat gambler. I never even knew him."

Raider didn't want to quit. He was still waiting for his chance. "Galler took you in. Treated you good. And you turned on him."

"He laid on top of me," she replied, her face blushing red. "That's all men want to do. You're no different. If I went with you, you'd stab me in the back."

"If you didn't stab me first."

She sighed. "This is all getting to be tiresome. Where the hell is Hardy with that rope?"

Raider took one careful step toward her as she glanced in the direction of the door. Too far to lunge. If he could just get close enough.

She looked back at him. "See what I mean. You want me, don't you. Only you want to see me hanging at the end of a rope."

"Ain't so sure they hang women in Idaho. Although in your case, they might make an exception."

"Nobody's going to hang me, Pinkerton. Not ever. I'll be the queen of this territory. You hear me? I'll have everything that's coming to me. And no man will stand in my way."

She was the worst kind of woman, Raider thought. Demanding like all females, but no conscience to temper her desires. He had seen it before, but never this bad. He had to bring her to justice. But how? He wasn't sure he had it in him to kill a woman, even one as ruthless as Cynthia Galler.

Morgan returned with a coil of strong rope. "Make him put his hands behind his back, Cindy."

"Go on," the girl commanded. "Do like he said."

Raider obliged, laughing in the bargain. "Mebbe you wanna tie me up with her apron strings, Hardy. She seems to have you tangled in 'em."

"We'll see who's laughing when we're through with you," Morgan said.

Raider couldn't understand how a man could let a woman give him orders. All along he had suspected that Hardy Morgan, alias Hunt Kreeger, wasn't very strong. The damned woman had caught him off guard though. After all, there hadn't been anything to suggest she was in charge. He had thought Cynthia Galler was the victim. The big man just hoped he wouldn't pay too badly for his error in judgment.

CHAPTER TWENTY

With his own gun pointed at his back, Raider walked down the steps to a cellar door in back of the building. They were going to lock him up in a deep, dark hole. Keep him captive like an animal. At least they hadn't killed him yet.

"Open the door," Cynthia Galler said.

Morgan obeyed her. His hands seemed to be trembling. Not much to him inside. Maybe Hardy was the weak link in the chain, the chance that Raider was waiting for. Of course, he would have to wait until the woman wasn't around. What a tough, wretched little bird, leveling the Colt at him.

"Should we tie his feet?" Morgan asked.

"Yes, after he's in the cellar."

Raider thought about moving right then. Butting Morgan to the ground, then going after the girl. Stomp them both to death. Best to wait. He was pretty sure the girl would get a bullet in him if he tried anything.

She waved toward the door with the barrel of his revolver. "If you don't go down those steps, I'll kill you immediately."

He decided to go down the steps. Morgan followed to finish hog-tying him.

The cellar was so small that he had to crouch. Having his hands behind him made him uncomfortable. He was trying to find a way to sit that wasn't painful as the doors started to close from above.

"Morgan!" he called as the dandy left him trussed up.

The doors stopped halfway. "What?"

"I forgot t' tell you somethin'," the big man offered.

"What?"

"Kiss my ass, you gopher-dicked asshole!"

Cool air stirred as the door plunked down.

Raider turned on his side, hoping there was some way to cut loose the ropes that held him. Something ran over his legs. Probably a pack rat. One of Morgan's kin. He sat in the dark, squirming, thinking thoughts that otherwise would have never crossed his mind.

Raider stirred, opening his eyes, trying to remember where he was. At first he was afraid the sickness had come back to his head, but then the whole thing focused. As he was sorting it out, the noise continued on the doors to the cellar. The tapping had awakened him in the first place. How long had he been out?

The tapping continued, followed by a weak voice. "Pinkerton!"

Raider wasn't sure he recognized the tone. "Yeah?" Had Morgan come back to torment him?

The cellar doors opened. It was still dark outside so Raider could not see the face as the man came in. Slow shuffling on the steps. Man moving like he was in pain.

Raider wondered if his old friend had come back from the grave. "Red Bear? That you?"

"No, it's me. Galler."

Raider would settle for the other old man. "Untie me, Galler. Come on, hurry. Here, let me turn so you can reach the knot."

Galler started to work on the ropes.

"How the hell did you get free anyway?" Raider asked.

"Talked Kreeger into untyin' me. Then I managed to cork him on the head. Got to get out of here before he wakes up."

"Morgan bought it, huh?"

"He's a dumb son of a bitch no matter what name he goes by. There, I think I got it."

Raider's hands were free. He rubbed his wrists, trying to

bring the feeling back into his arms. "Where's the girl?"

Galler shrugged. "Don't know."

"Probably hidin' under some rock."

Raider glared at the old man in the darkness. "That true what she said, 'bout you tappin' her?"

A deep sigh from Galler. "She came to my bed, Raider. I didn't want it that way. At least not at first. But she has a way of—"

Raider waved him off. "You don't have t' say no more."

"I want to talk about it," Galler said. "I fell in love with her. It wasn't wrong. She wasn't my blood."

"She probably just wanted t' make sure you didn't get rid o' her after her maw died."

A deep sigh from the old man. "When this Kreeger came along—"

"I know all about it," Raider replied. "Burden was in on ever'thin' with the girl an' Morgan. They killed him because he was too greedy."

"How—" Galler faltered, his voice on the edge of cracking. "How could they do that to me?"

Raider felt the strength returning to his arms. He reached down to untie his legs. "We can talk 'bout that later, ol' buddy. Right now we gotta get t' the sheriff."

Galler nodded. "I'll go up to make sure the coast is clear."

Raider figured he had to get to the lawman first. Tell him what had happened. Find the girl. Get Galler to testify against her and Morgan. The sheriff owed him a favor for killing Esky Pilot.

He started for the steps.

Galler had already ascended.

Raider was on the first step when the shotgun exploded.

Galler fell back into the hole with him, almost knocking Raider into the wall. The big man pushed Galler aside. He bent down to feel the man's chest, at least what was left of it.

Someone appeared above him. "Don't try it, Pinkerton."

The girl had returned.

She called to Morgan. "Get down there and tie him up again, you dumb bastard. Go on. He won't bite you."

Raider glared up at her with eyes as black as the night. "I wouldn't be so sure o' that, woman."

Morgan hesitated. "Cindy—"

Raider wondered if she had used both barrels of the scattergun on her stepfather. Maybe he should just charge; knock them both down. He was getting pretty tired of their shenanigans.

She seemed to read his mind. "I've got one barrel left," she said through clenched teeth. "Come out of there if you want to die like the old man. Come on, you bastard."

Morgan whined again. "Cindy—I thought we agreed we weren't going to kill him right away."

"Shut up, Hardy! I'll blow his head off if he moves an inch. What'll it be, Pinkerton? Have you got the guts?"

Raider had only one option. He had to surrender. No way could he take on the scattergun; not head on. Best to stay alive for now, wait for a better opportunity. He held out his wrists, as if he wanted them to be tied.

"Good," Cynthia Galler said. "You're smarter than I thought."

Hardy Morgan moved down to tie his hands. Raider glared at the man's skinny neck. Just wrap his hands around Morgan's throat, choke the life out of him. Or use him as a shield against the woman.

Morgan stopped. "Make him turn around, Cindy."

Raider wanted to grab him right then.

The woman motioned with the barrel of the shotgun. "Turn around, Pinkerton. Go on, or you'll get it in the chest."

Raider turned his back to her. "Why don't you plug me now? Hell, shootin' a man in the back wouldn't be much t' you."

"Shut up!" she cried. "Do you hear me! Hardy, is he tied yet?"

Raider felt the cold clink of manacles around his wrists. Cynthia Galler must have gone for the chains herself. She realized the big man would be a problem for them if he had any chance at all of escaping. The chains were insurance for the hateful couple.

Cynthia Galler looked to her left. "Hardy, I hear somebody coming. I have to close the doors."

Good, Raider thought as the doors slammed shut, he had a shot in the dark. Lean on Morgan, shove him against the wall, head butt him until his brians flowed into the cool earth. Then he felt the barrel of a small revolver against his ribs.

"You move once, Pinkerton, and I'll kill you as sure as I'm standing here. Understand?"

Raider was filled with rage. A woman and a tenderfoot were getting the best of him. He held his tongue, though. The gun had to be respected.

They could hear Cynthia Galler outside as she talked to the sheriff.

"What seems to be the trouble, Miss Galler? That's a mighty big gun for such a little lady."

She turned on the tears. "Oh, Sheriff, it's those darned rats again. I just get so afraid of them. I thought if I came out here with a shotgun, I might be able to scare them off."

The lawman assumed a fatherly tone. "Now, now, Cindy, you know you can't be shootin' at night in these here town limits. Why, that's just the kind of thing we're discouragin'. If Idaho is ever gonna get statehood, we've got to stop these goin's on."

Her voice was penitent. "I'm so sorry, Sheriff. You know I'm a law-abiding citizen. Why, I don't know what my father would say. I wish he was here to help me."

"Is he still down in Boise?" the sheriff asked.

"Yes, sir. I wish he was here to help me. Why, I don't know what I'd do without Mr. Morgan."

The sheriff chuckled a little. "Well, we're just happy to have two fine people like you and Mr. Morgan as citizens. I'm hopin' to hear weddin' bells for y'all real soon."

"Oh, Sheriff, how you do go on!"

Raider exhaled the stale air of the cellar. "Sugar wouldn't melt in her little mouth."

Morgan dug the gun into his ribs. "Shut up," he whispered.

"You ain't gonna shoot me, Hardy, not with the sheriff out there."

"Try me," Morgan replied.

Outside, the sheriff was ready to leave. "Okay, Miss Cynthia, you be careful with that scattergun."

"I will, Sheriff."

"And if you have more trouble with rats, see the blacksmith. He's pretty good at getting rid of those things."

"Surely. Good night, Sheriff."

After a few minutes, the doors to the cellar swung open again.

"That was a close one," said Hardy Morgan.

He left Raider, starting up the steps.

Cynthia Galler gazed down at the big man. "We should kill him now."

Raider glared back her. "Suits me fine."

"Cindy," Morgan whined. "I told you that we need him. He's worth more to us alive."

She sighed. "All right. But we move tonight. I don't want to wait any longer. It's too risky."

"What about the old man?" Morgan asked.

"We'll bury him along the way."

Morgan nodded. "Fine."

"Now shut those doors till we're ready."

Raider watched as the doors slammed again.

He looked down at the dead boy, wondering if they were going to make him dig the grave. How could she kill her stepfather? And how long would it be before she killed the big man from Arkansas?

CHAPTER TWENTY-ONE

When the cellar doors opened again, Raider looked up to see Hardy Morgan's shadow coming down the steps. The girl was right behind him. She had the shotgun in hand. Raider wondered if she would use the scattergun when she finally decided to kill him. If he was lucky, the shot would be a clean one, kill him quickly.

"Stay where you are," Morgan said.

Raider heard the clinking of chains.

Morgan reached down to take off the big man's boots. Raider drew back and kicked him straight into the wall. Morgan grunted as the breath left his lungs. Raider moved to stand up. It was his last chance.

The girl stopped him with the shotgun. "Not another inch," she said.

Raider stared at the double-eyed bore of the weapon.

"Go on," Cynthia Galler challenged. "I'd love to blow your head off right now. Go on."

"Tell the sheriff that it's rats again?" Raider replied. "Or would he just think that the Galler girl is at it again?"

"Take another step if you want to find out."

Raider stood dead still. "There's somethin' I wanna know,

Cindy. Why'd you wait so long t' kill Burden and t' kidnap your paw?"

"Circumstances," she replied. "It just worked out that way. And Sheriff King and your four friends kept us busy. Although I daresay not as busy as you've kept us, Raider. You've been a thorn to us. I ought to give you both barrels right now. I'm sure it would save us a lot of trouble in the long run."

Hardy Morgan stood up, catching his breath. "No! Don't kill him. Unless he tries something like that again. Then let him have it."

Raider tried to laugh. "Hardy, are you gettin' t' be my pal?"

"No, Pinkerton," the breathless man replied. "I hate you as much as Cindy. I just want to see you pay for that little rough-house. And believe me, you'll pay dearly. Now sit down again and let me take off those boots."

They were going to leave him shoeless. But he had to obey. Keep his temper in check. Hope the right moment would come.

When his boots were off, Morgan fastened the manacles around his ankles.

"All right," the girl said. "Get him up here."

Morgan told the big man to stand again. Slowly Raider got to his feet. It was hard walking in the chains, but he managed to make it up the steps. The girl kept her distance, pointing the scattergun at him.

She motioned to a waiting buckboard. "Into the wagon."

Raider climbed on the back of the buckboard. "Takin' me home?"

"Shut up," the girl said. "Lie down. Go on, do as I say. Lie down or I'll give you both barrels."

Raider sighed, shaking his head. He crawled into the wagon, reclining on the floor of the buckboard. They put the body of Robert Galler next to him and then covered the wagon with a canvas tarp that they tied tightly in place. They trussed up the rear too. No way to escape. Not as long as he was hemmed in.

Morgan and the girl mounted the driver's seat and started forward. Raider and the dead man bounced with every rock and pothole that caught the wagon wheels, until they stopped to bury Galler. At least they didn't make Raider dig the grave. He bounced alone when they drove on. A hell of a ride. But so far, it was better than dying.

When the wagon could go no farther, they transferred Raider to the back of a packhorse. He had to ride belly-down, tied on the animal the same way that he always tied prisoners. Not a good way to travel. And all the time the girl was right there on her mount, holding the shotgun.

Someone else joined them on the trail, a big, scar-faced Shoshone, a man who resembled the Indian Raider had killed on the mountain. Morgan wasted no time telling Raider that the new Shoshone was the brother of the dead man. And he wasn't happy about losing his kin; that he aimed to make Raider pay.

"That just makes my day," Raider said, trying to sound cocky.

The Shoshone swung the butt of a Winchester rifle, catching Raider in the ribs. The big man grunted, vowing to himself to keep his mouth shut. He had a feeling that they weren't taking him to a barn dance.

"Don't hurt him too badly," Morgan said. "I want him ready to work in the mine."

So that was it. They planned to use Raider's muscle to look for the big vein of silver, the mother lode. As much as he hated mining, Raider was now hopeful for his chances. He was alive. And he had gotten out of worse predicaments in his time.

When they reached the mining encampment, Morgan and the girl wasted no time putting him to work. They stripped him of everything but his pants and then told him to get into the harness at the end of the long rope. The Shoshone stood ready to pull him up to the adit.

"Why'd you start diggin' so far up?" the big man asked.

Morgan shrugged. "You'd never understand the reasons."

"That's right," the girl intoned. "Hardy knows about these things. He says there's a vein up there and I believe him."

"You sure 'bout that?" Raider replied with a coyote grin.

Morgan cleared his throat. "Yes."

The girl glared at her beau. "There better be a vein in this mountain."

"There is, honey. I assure you."

Cynthia gestured to the Indian. "Pull him up."

Raider started to ascend on the line. When he was halfway up, the Shoshone let him fall a few feet. Then he stopped the descent, laughing at his joke. Raider tried to catch his breath, hating the Indian and his captors.

"You'd better not slack off!" Morgan yelled from below. "We're going to check your work."

Good, Raider thought. If Morgan was going to send somebody up to look at the mine, then that meant Raider would be coming down. He'd have to wait for the right opening. But then he would move. And he didn't care if he died in the process. He just wanted to go out like a man.

His arms and hands ached.

For a week, he had been doing the same thing. Working all day, into the night. They'd bring him down, give him a plate of slop and let him sleep in the bunkhouse for a few hours. Then they'd get him up at dawn again, make him start back to work.

The mine was getting bigger inside. While Raider slept, Morgan sent a man up to look at his progress. It was the same man who had been working before. He would stay in the mine for a couple of hours, chiseling and hammering to keep the operation going around the clock.

Morgan and the girl would always wait at the base of the cliff, expecting news of a strike. Each morning, they were disappointed. Raider could see that the woman was getting antsy, wondering if she had bet on the wrong horse. The big man thought he could use that to his advantage.

Of course, it didn't matter much that they left him alone in the bunkhouse. The Shoshone always chained him to the bed while Cynthia Galler stood by with her scattergun. Even if he had been able to walk, he wouldn't have been able to drag the bed very far.

So the torture went on. Working like an animal, hammering in the guts of the mountain. Raider prayed that he didn't strike a vein of silver. He was pretty sure they would kill him after he struck pay dirt.

• • •

He seemed to be getting weaker. Inside the mine, he would have to take longer breaks. Sometimes the Indian would fire his rifle if the hammering stopped for too long. Raider knew he was going to have to move soon. If his body failed him, he wouldn't have a chance.

After the second week, he would return to the bunkhouse and flop on the cornshuck mattress. His head spun, his heart pounded. Maybe being dead was better than this. Maybe— Stop the crazy thoughts, he told himself. Shape up. Get your head straight. Don't give up. Not as long as he was breathing.

"You look to be a sight," a strange voice said.

Raider lifted his head. His black eyes focused on the old man who sat across the room in the wooden chair. It was all over. Now he was starting to hallucinate. He'd probably lose what was left of his mind soon enough.

"Those chains don't look good on you," Red Bear said.

Raider laid his head down. "Go away, old man. You're dead. Cindy and Morgan done killed you."

Red Bear laughed. "They left me for dead. But I'm not. I been holed up in the mountains."

"Get these chains off me," Raider said.

Red Bear shook his head. "I can't. It wouldn't do any good. You've got to make your own way."

Raider sighed, shaking his head. "Thanks a lot."

"Don't mention it."

"Maybe you are a spook after all," the big man offered. "Came back to haunt me."

Red Bear got out of the chair and limped toward him. "Can a spook give you food? Here, eat this."

He held a big hunk of venison in front of Raider. It was warm, fresh off the spit. Raider ate until his belly ached.

Red Bear limped back to his chair.

"They hurt you pretty bad?" Raider asked.

The Shoshone shrugged. "I reckon. It just shows you the white man ain't good at nothin'. They couldn't even kill me right."

Raider looked up at the ceiling. "What am I gonna do?"

"Find silver," Red Bear offered.

"Right. That's when they kill me."

"Or when you kill them," the Indian offered.

"What?"

Red Bear chortled. "Do I have to figure it all out for you?"

The big man started to figure it. "You might have somethin' there, Red Bear. I think I see what you mean."

"You know somethin', Raider. You're mighty smart. For a white man."

Raider closed his eyes. Could he pull it off? The venison had helped. His strength might return now. He wanted to thank Red Bear but he fell asleep.

When the big Shoshone returned to take him to the mine, Red Bear was gone.

Raider walked to the edge of the adit and waved. "Silver!" he cried. "A big vein."

He watched as Morgan and the girl urged the big Indian into the harness. Would they have the strength to pull the Shoshone to the entrance of the mine? Slowly the Indian rose toward the adit, coming closer with his Winchester. Morgan didn't have the guts to come himself. But it made no difference to Raider. He would move on the Shoshone first and then round up the hateful couple.

When the Indian pulled himself onto the ledge, Raider motioned into the heart of the mine. "Big vein," he said. "Hurry."

The Indian pushed past him, stepping into the shadows.

Raider jumped from behind, wrapping his chains around the Shoshone's throat, using all his power to strangle Morgan's henchman.

The Indian was strong. He wheeled around and around, trying to knock Raider against the walls of the mine, trying to dislodge the big Pinkerton from his throat. But it was no good. Raider held on until the Shoshone fell dead to the floor.

Raider grabbed the rifle and walked to the edge of the mine's entrance. He looked down at Morgan and the girl, whose faces were turned expectantly to the sky. Raider levered the rifle, aiming at their heads.

"Surprise," he said to himself.

When the rifle barked, Morgan and the girl started to run.

Raider fired the Winchester two more times but they were out of range. He couldn't get the angle on them, not so high up. He'd have to go down and chase them. He reached for the rope, tying it fast to the block and tackle above him. It was hard climbing down with the rifle, but he managed to touch his bare feet to the ground in a few minutes.

He looked up to see Morgan and his girl galloping away on a pair of horses. And Raider had a pretty good idea where they were going. He just hoped he could catch them before they caused any more harm.

CHAPTER TWENTY-TWO

Raider hurried to the white tent where Morgan had been camped. He found a pair of boots and some more ammunition for the rifle. Maybe they weren't headed where he thought. Maybe they were just riding off in the same direction. Just like a couple of chickens to turn tail and run when things went in the other direction.

In back of the bunkhouse he saw the old mule tied to a hitching post. The animal was munching on a pile of hay. Raider put a bridle over the mule's head. The mule didn't like it much when Raider climbed on its bare back. It bucked until it realized that Raider had no intention of dismounting.

"Hyah!"

The ride was bumpy but Raider managed to hang on.

He slowed the animal when he got to the creek. The tracks from Morgan's mount ended at the water. They had turned north, toward Lonnegan's place. Maybe they wouldn't threaten Cassie and her father.

Raider knew better. Cynthia Galler had mocked him about Cassie. And it was just like Robert Galler's stepdaughter to take advantage of the weak link in the chain. Raider urged the animal into the creek, riding as fast as he could along the bed of the stream.

The wind blew in his face. He held the rifle in his gun hand. It felt right to have the weapon, to be riding headlong into the fray. This was the way he wanted it to be. His best chance.

He just hoped the girl and her father came out of it all right.

When he rounded the bend, he saw Morgan's horses tied up in front of the Lonnegan place. Smoke rose from the chimney. They were inside. He looked toward Homer Lonnegan's mine, wondering if the old man had gone back to work. Had he recovered from his belly wound enough to go back to digging?

The door of the cabin opened.

Hardy Morgan came out for a look-see.

He seemed to think the coast was clear.

When he had gone back inside, Raider started running for the house. His body had come to life again. Red Bear's venison had done it. And killing the Shoshone had filled him with a new rage.

He slipped up to the corner of the cabin, hesitating, listening. Voices rose inside. Cassie Lonnegan was begging them not to hurt her father. She told them to take her as hostage, but leave the old man alone.

Raider eased next to the window, peering in. Cynthia Galler held Raider's Colt in her hand. She had the weapon trained on Cassie Lonnegan. Hardy Morgan stood next to her with the shotgun ready.

Cassie had begun to cry. "Please," she said. "Don't hurt him."

"Hah!" the Galler woman replied. "If the Pilot cousins had done their job, you'd both be dead. That damned Pinkerton was the one who caused all of this. And he's sweet on you, honey. So you're coming along with us for insurance."

"Yes," Cassie said. "Anything. Just don't hurt my father."

Morgan seemed to be anxious to leave. "Cindy, he's going to come after us. We'd better hurry."

"Shut up, you weakling. Do you think that Pinkerton is going to shoot at us when we have this little tramp as a shield?"

"No," Morgan replied, "but we'd better leave. I want to

get back to Boise so we can file that claim. I mean, the Pinkerton did discover a vein."

Cynthia glared at her beau. "You fool! Raider didn't discover any silver. He just said that so we'd send the Indian up."

"How the hell did he overpower that Shoshone? We weren't feeding him enough to make him strong."

"It doesn't matter," his murderous sweetheart replied. "We have to get the hell out of here."

Cassie stared wide-eyed at her tormenters. "Then Raider is alive?"

Cynthia Galler slapped her face. "Yes, he's—"

Raider enjoyed what happened next. Cassie jumped on the Galler woman, wrestling her to the floor of the cabin. They tussled for a few seconds until Morgan pulled them apart.

"You little whore!" cried Cynthia Galler.

Cassie jumped to her feet. "You're the whore! You almost killed my father. And if I had a gun, I'd kill you!"

A haughty smile from the hateful woman. "But you don't have a gun, do you? In fact, you don't have a chance. As soon as we get away, we're going to kill you."

"I don't care what you do to me," Cassie replied. "But please don't hurt my father."

Cynthia Galler gestured toward the bedroom. "Go in and blow his brains out, Hardy. Go on, do like I tell you!"

Raider felt his gut churning. He couldn't stand by while Morgan killed Homer Lonnegan. He should have gone in while the girls were wrestling. It had happened too quickly. Now he'd have to take the chance that Cassie might get caught in the cross fire.

Hardy Morgan hesitated. "Kill him?"

"You heard me! Do it now!"

Morgan shook his head. "Cindy, I don't want to."

She glared at him. "Don't disobey me, Hardy. Defiance doesn't look good on you."

"I won't, Cindy. I won't kill him!"

Raider held his breath. If they would just come outside—but if Morgan went into the bedroom, he'd have to move. Damn it all, did he really love the Lonnegan girl so much? He owed her and her father after they had saved his ass.

Morgan stood his ground. "I refuse to do it, Cindy. I won't kill him. If you want him dead, you'll have to do it yourself."

"No!" Cassie cried. "Kill me instead."

"You're both fools!" the Galler woman cried.

Morgan gestured toward the door. "Cindy, we have to go."

"Yes," she said. "But don't give me orders, Hardy. Let this be the last time you talk back to me."

"All right, Cindy! But let's go!"

"And don't raise your voice to me, you worm. Do you understand!"

"I don't want to hang," Morgan said. "And if that Pinkerton catches us, that's exactly what will happen."

"All right! All right!"

Raider eased away from the window. He levered the rifle, wondering if he would get a clean shot. He didn't want to hurt Cassie but he also didn't want Morgan and the woman to run any farther.

"Hurry, Cindy."

"Come on, bitch. You'll lead the way."

Cassie was in front of them when they came through the door.

Raider wheeled around, lowering the rifle. "That's far enough!"

Cynthia Morgan grabbed Cassie's hair and put the gun to her head. She held Cassie between her and the rifle. Morgan slid in behind both of the women. It seemed like a standoff.

"Drop it, woman," Raider urged.

"Do you think I'm a fool?" Cynthia Galler cried.

Raider nodded. "Yep. An' I think a whole lot more that's worse. Now put the gun on the ground an' back away. You too, Hardy."

The Galler woman laughed. "You won't shoot. Not with Miss Blue Eyes between me and the bullet. Now you back off!"

"Don't do it, Raider!" Cassie cried. "Kill both of them. Don't worry about me."

Cassie cried out as Cynthia Galler pulled her hair.

"He won't shoot," she cried. "Can't you see, honey? He's in love with you. He wants to marry you."

Raider hesitated with the rifle. Maybe she was right. Maybe he did love Cassie Lonnegan. But it didn't matter. He wouldn't shoot even if he didn't love her. He lowered the Winchester.

"All right," the big man said. "Clear on out."

A smile from the hateful woman. "I knew you were smart, Raider. Hardy, get the horses."

Morgan just stood there.

"Hardy!"

Morgan eased back toward the mounts. He climbed up into the saddle, gazing down at the woman who held the Colt to Cassie's head. What the hell was he going to do? Raider watched, waiting for the right time to move.

"Bring the horses, Hardy!" She did not look back at him. "Hardy!"

"I'm sorry, Cindy," Morgan replied. "I'm afraid I have to part ways with you here."

"What?"

Morgan held the shotgun against his hip with the barrel raised toward the sky. "I'm leaving you, Cindy. If I stay with you any longer, I'm sure to hang. This way, maybe I have a chance to escape. Good-bye, Cindy, I'm—"

Raider flinched when he heard the Colt explode. Cynthia Galler had turned quickly to fire a shot into Hardy Morgan's chest. Morgan fell from the horse, convulsing on the ground. Before Raider could do anything, Cynthia Galler had the smoking gun pointed at Cassie's head again.

"Don't try it, Pinkerton, or I put a bullet through Miss Blue Eyes's skull."

She started backing toward the horse.

Raider lifted the rifle again. "Give it up, Cindy. I'm gonna find you sooner or later."

"No you won't."

He couldn't get off a shot without hitting Cassie.

"You cain't run," he offered. "This terr'tory ain't big 'nough for you t' hide in. I found you once, I'll find you again."

"Don't let her take me, Raider," Cassie cried.

The hateful woman pulled her hair again. "Shut up, you little bitch. I'd kill you right now if you weren't so useful to me."

Raider thought he might fire off a round, get the Galler woman in the head. He had always balked at killing women, but maybe now it was time to make an exception. But he couldn't hit Cassie.

"All right," he said. "Just go. An' don't worry, Cassie, I'll be right—"

He flinched again.

A shotgun exploded behind the two women.

Cynthia Galler buckled, falling forward on top of Cassie.

Raider gazed down to see Hardy Morgan propped up on one arm. He had fired both barrels into Cynthia's back. Raider pointed the rifle at him, but Morgan collapsed again, slumping facedown into the dirt.

Sweat broke instantly on Raider's forehead.

Had the shotgun blast gone clear through the Galler woman?

Had Cassie taken a load of shot in her own back?

When he rolled Cynthia Galler off Cassie, the blue eyes turned up to him.

"Raider?" She had blood on her but it belonged to the other woman.

He lifted her into his arms. "It's all right, Cassie."

She began to cry hysterically.

Raider picked her up and carried her inside the house.

Homer Lonnegan called out from the bedroom. "What the devil's goin' on out there?"

Raider carried Cassie into the bedroom. "It's over now, Mr. Lonnegan. Your daughter is all right."

Lonnegan began to cry. "Thank God. Thank God."

Raider put Cassie on the bed next to him. "Take care of her until I get the mess cleaned up outside."

"Why?" Homer Lonnegan asked. "Why did they want to hurt us?"

The big man shook his head. "Try not to think on it, Homer. It will drive you crazy if you do."

The old man put his arms around his daughter. "Thank you Raider."

"Sure, Homer. Sure."

He went back outside to look at the bodies.

He owed Hardy Morgan for saving him the trouble of killing the woman.

His head went to work, thinking like a Pinkerton. Get the sheriff from Cascade. Tell him the whole story. Bury the bodies. Send a wire to the agency. Write his report.

Looking down at the body of Hardy Morgan, he thought it

was strange that the man waited until he was half dead before he stood up to Cynthia Galler.

The sight made his stomach turn.

He went back inside, finding the jug that Lonnegan kept hidden in the floor of the cabin. The liquid burned as it went down. Raider shook off the fire that spread over him.

He took another drink, wondering how long it would be before he felt right again.

CHAPTER TWENTY-THREE

Homer Lonnegan gazed at the big Pinkerton from Arkansas. "That scar's healed up pretty good," he said. "When the hair grows back, you probably won't even be able to see it."

Cassie frowned at her father. "Papa, it's not polite to talk about such things at the dinner table."

Lonnegan winked at her. "Sorry, honey."

A smile cracked the big man's lips. "Aw, don't fret, Cassie. I ain't takin' no offense."

"Well I am!" the girl replied. "I don't care if you two choose to act like savages. I'm still a civilized person and while you're in my house, I expect you to be the same."

Lonnegan exchanged smiles with Raider. They were both happy to see the girl perked up for a change. She had been right mopey since the unfortunate trouble with the Galler woman. It had taken her almost a week to come out of it, but now she seemed herself again.

"More potatoes?" she asked Raider.

She had cooked a big dinner for them.

Raider shook his head. "No thank you, Cassie. I'm just about as full as I can get."

Cassie was offering her father another helping of meat when the knock resounded on the door.

Raider stood up, reaching for the Colt at his side. "I'll git it."

Cassie frowned at the weapon. "Raider—"

Homer Lonnegan stopped his daughter. "Let him be, Cassie."

When Raider flung open the door, he leveled the Colt at Red Bear.

"Hmm," the old Shoshone said, "I guess this means I'm not invited to dinner."

Raider holstered the weapon. "Git in here, Red Bear."

Homer and Cassie welcomed him to the table.

Red Bear dug in like he had never had a decent meal in his life.

"Don't eat 'em outta house an' home," Raider warned.

Red Bear nodded. "Say, what happened with all of that foolishness? You know, with Morgan and the woman?"

"Thought you didn't take no notice o' the white man's doin's," Raider said.

Red Bear shrugged. "I'm curious. Like a otter with a turtle. I want to see what's inside the shell."

Homer Lonnegan gestured to Raider. "The big 'un here took care of it." He went on to tell about the standoff, about the way Morgan shot his sweetheart in the back. Red Bear continued to listen while he ate. None of it seemed to affect him much.

Raider watched Homer, trying to avoid the looks that Cassie had started to give him. He could see it in her face, the wanting. And she knew she couldn't have him, which made her want him even more.

"So you see," Lonnegan went on, "that Morgan saved ever'body a lot of trouble by pluggin' her himself."

"Hmm," Red Bear said. "I never trusted much in love."

"Neither does somebody else I know!" Cassie cried. She got up and started to clear the table.

Raider wanted to say something, but Lonnegan waved him off. "Let her stew a while," he said. "She'll cool down."

"After she seemed to be in such a good mood," Raider offered.

"Women are changeable," Lonnegan replied.

Red Bear reached out for the cornbread. "So what happened after Morgan got killed?"

"I went for the sheriff in Cascade," Raider replied. "He didn't b'lieve me till I showed him where they had buried Robert Galler. Took me a while t' find it myself. Then he accused me o' killin' Galler, which didn't make no sense. I had to drag him out here and have Mr. Lonnegan and Cassie tell him the truth."

Red Bear sighed. "Well, it worked out for the best I suppose."

"There's somethin' I ain't told yet," Raider said. "Somethin' that I want ever'body t' hear. Cassie, come in here."

She pouted a little, but she rejoined them at the table.

"What is it?" she asked. "Are you leaving?"

"Yes, but not till I tell you this."

He took a deep breath.

They were all staring at him.

"While I was in Cascade," he said, "I checked on all of the minin' stuff. Seems Galler really didn't have a claim on those digs. He had been pokin' 'round an' he even put up that sign Morgan painted over."

Cassie started to get up again. "We know all that."

Lonnegan shot his daughter a stern look. "Sit down, Cassie. Let Raider finish."

"Just this," the big man said. "When I called down t' tell Morgan that I found a vein, I wasn't lyin'."

"What?" Red Bear exclaimed.

Raider nodded. "That's right. I found a vein. It's gray an' as big around as a muskmelon. Should be worth a bunch t' anybody who's willin' to' climb up there an' dig it out."

"Whew," Lonnegan said. "Wish I had that kind of luck."

"Me too," Red Bear replied.

Cassie smirked at him. "Well, good for you."

"Hear me out," Raider rejoined. "I figgered since Galler was dead that the claim was rightly mine. I did find the vein after all."

"Oh, you did!" Cassie wailed, pointing a finger at him. "Now you're rich and we're still dirt-claimers!"

Raider reached into his shirt pocket, taking out a piece of paper. "I wish you wouldn't be so hard on me, Cassie. See, I filed the claim in the name of you and your paw."

Homer Lonnegan's eyes widened. "Don't play with me, Raider."

He tossed the paper in front of them. "Ain't playin'. There it is. You're on there too, Red Bear."

"Hmm," the Indian said, "I told you to leave somethin' for me, but this is better than I could have hoped for."

Raider exhaled, rising from the table. "Well, seein's how Cassie don't want me here no more, I reckon I better be goin'. Gotta write my report an' send it t' the home office. I gotta tell 'em where t' find the remains o' those five dead friends o' mine. In case their families wanna know."

Lonnegan rose with him. "Now look here, Raider. You're welcome to stay as long as you like."

He looked at the girl, who now seemed confused. "Cassie wants me t' go."

"No she don't."

"How 'bout it, Cassie?" the big man asked.

She lowered her face. "Well—"

"Aw, give him a break," her father entreated.

Red Bear was in agreement.

She lifted her blue eyes, smiling. "Oh, darn it. If I can't have a husband, I might as well have a silver mine. Sit down, you Pinkerton!"

Lonnegan clapped his hands. "Guess I'll have to get my jug."

Red Bear sighed. "Well, if I can't work for a white man, maybe I oughta be partners with one. Shake on it, Lonnegan?"

They shook and the old man ran to get his jug.

Cassie came back with cups for the corn liquor.

After a few drinks, they all began to laugh, recounting the exploits of the tall, black-eyed man who sat across the table from them.

CHAPTER TWENTY-FOUR

Allan Pinkerton looked up when William Wagner dropped the dusty envelope on his desk.

Pinkerton eyed the stained dispatch. "From Raider?"

Wagner nodded. "It just came in. We finally know what happened to the four men I sent to Idaho."

Pinkerton opened the envelope and read the report that Wagner had already perused. "My God," he said, lowering his head. "They're all dead."

"The girl was behind it all along," Wagner rejoined.

Pinkerton sighed. "Raider stopped the foolishness. And according to this, the responsible parties have paid for their crime. Ah—saints preserve us, William, that's not going to bring those boys back."

Wagner sighed, tears welling in his eyes. "No sir."

Pinkerton rose out of his leather chair. "I better tell the others."

He went into the main office and informed everyone that the four agents had died in the line of duty. He also told them that the deaths had been avenged by Raider, which brought a more favorable reaction. Pinkerton quieted them with a stern glance and then went back into his office.

Behind his desk, he picked up the letter from Raider. "He

gives directions to the area where they're buried. Says to see a man name of Red Bear or another one named Homer Lonnegan. I leave you to inform the families of those men, William. Tell them that we will assist in every way that we can. Do you understand?"

"Yes," Wagner replied sadly. "And after I do, I hope you'll accept my resignation from this agency."

Pinkerton looked startled. "I beg your pardon?"

"I have no choice," Wagner offered. "I'm responsible for the deaths of those men."

"They died in the line of duty," Pinkerton replied. "You sent them to a task. They knew the risk involved."

"I sent them!" Wagner said. "They went because I told them to. Four of them, Allan!"

Pinkerton sighed. "I can't let you resign over somethin' like this. William. I won't accept your quittin'."

"But—"

"You're not a quitter, William. Neither is Raider. Look here. He's takin' some time off. He's earned it. Why don't you do the same?"

"Time off to look for another line of work?"

Pinkerton pointed a finger at him. "There is no other line of work for you, lad. Stay on here, where you're needed."

"Four men, Allan. And I'm responsible."

"We're not perfect," the big Scotsman offered. "Nor are the soldiers we send into battle. A general loses men, William. It's the cost of war."

Wagner took a deep breath. "Is that what we are? Generals?"

"That's as close as I can come to an answer, William. If you want to leave my employ, then you're free to go. But don't expect me to like it. You've been too valuable to me."

Four men, Wagner thought. He should have sent two men as a team after the first one disappeared. He wondered if the Pinkerton killers would have defeated a team. They hadn't been able to kill Raider.

"Take some time off," Pinkerton entreated. "Follow Raider's example for once."

"No, I don't think so."

"Then you're quittin'?"

Wagner shook his head. "No. I'm going back to my desk.

I'm going to write letters to the families of those four men. I'm going to tell them how sorry I am that they had to die."

"It's for the best, William."

Wagner nodded. What was it that Raider always called his assignments? Chicken-pickin' jobs? Wagner figured they were both in the same boat. Chicken-pickin' jobs. Those were the only kind of jobs that he and Raider deserved.

EPILOGUE

Raider rapped twice on the door of the white house.

A black woman opened the door and peered out at him with suspicious eyes. "Whatchoo want?" she demanded.

"Lookin' for Rosey," the big man replied. "Somebody told me she lived here. Sure is a nice house, too. Pretty yard. And them flowers is nice."

"Who are you?" the black woman asked.

"Name's Raider. Hey, I don't want no trouble. I just come lookin' for Rosey. If she ain't here, I'm on my way."

"Hold on a minute," the woman said.

She closed the door and went back into the house.

Raider waited for a while until the door flew open again.

Rosey grinned from ear to ear. "Damn you, Raider! How come you took so long gettin' back to Kansas?"

The big man shrugged. "Been busy, Rosey. Mind if I come in?"

She stepped out of the way. "Come on in, boy. You're gonna love it."

Raider had to admit that it was a nice house.

Rosey brought the black woman out to meet him. "Lilah, this is the man I was tellin' you about. Gave me the rest of the money I needed to buy this place."

"Glory be," Lilah said. "It's Mr. Raider hisself."

Raider took off his Stetson. "None other."

Lilah started toward the kitchen. "I gotta cook somethin' special tonight. Got to feed this big man."

Rosey kissed him on the cheek. Then she frowned, brushing back the long hair that hung down over his ears. "You got a fresh scar."

"Ain't that fresh," Raider said, removing her hand. "How come women always gotta look at your wounds?"

"So we can make them better."

Raider said the scar had healed a long time ago.

"You want coffee?" Rosey asked. "Or whiskey?"

"Whiskey will do just fine."

She led him into a big parlor where he sat down on a new sofa.

Rosey poured him some fine Irish whiskey. It didn't burn at all.

Rosey sat down next to him. "Ain't it grand, Raider? And you helped me. I never would've been able to do it without you."

He sighed, looking at the floor. "Don't fret, honey. That money woulda gone t' some slick faro dealer."

"I thought you hated faro."

"I do."

Rosey looked sideways at him. "What's wrong with you? You look like a bear cub that's done lost his momma."

"There was this girl," he started. "Her name was Cassie—"

He told her about the adventure in Idaho. Seems he hadn't realized how much he had cared about the girl until he left. Then he got a letter from her, came through the agency, telling him how she had found another man and was getting married. The silver mine was doing well for the Lonnegans and they wanted him to attend the wedding.

"Did you go?" Rosey asked.

"No. But it made me sad. I reckon I'm just stupid, Rosey. I turned down silver an' a good woman."

She put her arm around his shoulder. "Now, Raider, you know that you wouldn't be happy with some dreamy-eyed bride. It might be fun for a while, but you'd get tired of it."

"What about the silver?"

"Aw, you think gold and silver is both bad luck. Don't you?"

The big man nodded. "I still feel like I been et by a wolf an' shit off a cliff. I can't remember when I was this low."

"Lower'n a gopher's ass, eh?"

He glanced at her. "Where'd you hear that one?"

"From you."

He exhaled dejectedly. "Rosey, when I gave you that money, you said I had a lifetime of freebies comin' t' me."

She kissed him lightly on the cheek. "That you do, cowboy. After we eat, I'll give you a bath and take you upstairs. See, I'm operatin' again. I got a little Mexican filly that'll make you forget that Lonnegan girl in a minute."

"Aw, that's all right. I've swore off women for a while. Just let me stay the night an' git some sleep. Then we'll be even."

"Okay," she replied. "But you got to take a bath. I ain't havin' you stinkin' up my sheets!"

"Whatever you say, Rosey."

He had to admit that the fried chicken dinner was good. Lilah also served grits and collard greens. He ate until his stomach bulged out.

"Reckon I'll have that bath now," he said.

"There's a tub in the bathhouse out back," Rosey replied. "Only it ain't a real bathhouse, just a shed."

"Don't matter," Raider said. "Just as long as it's a real tub."

Out back, he eased into the tub of cold water. Summer was almost over. Wouldn't be able to bathe like this much longer. He was soaping himself when the doe-eyed Mexican girl walked in.

Raider glared at her. "What're you doin' here?"

She dropped her dress, standing naked before him. Small, brown-tipped breasts, long black hair, curly patch between her brown thighs. She came to the edge of the tub and smiled at him.

"Rosey sent me," she said.

Raider waved her off. "Ain't cottonin' t' no women right now. Mebbe if you can—"

She took the soap away from him and started to wash his back.

"You're a big man," she said.

Raider sighed. "Mebbe. I—"

Her hands went down his chest, to his stomach.

"My name is Juana," the girl said.

She touched his prick, which immediately came to life.

"Juana, huh? That's a pretty name."

Raider suddenly felt a lot better. He tried to remember what he had been sad about but it wouldn't come back to him. So he reached up and pulled the girl over into the tub with him.

Immediately, Juana grabbed his cock and guided it to the wet lips of her cunt. "You're so big," she cooed.

But when she sat on him, she was able to accommodate his entire length.

They splashed in the water until Raider discharged inside her.

"Thanks, honey," he said, kissing her. "You sure are sweet."

"So am I," another voice said.

Rosey stood naked as a jaybird in the shed. She climbed into the tub, kissing Raider and then kissing the Mexican girl. Juana touched Rosey's breast, rubbing her nipple.

"That feels good, sugar," Rosey said.

Juana lowered her mouth to Rosey's nipple.

Raider felt himself getting hard again.

Rosey reached for his crotch. "We're gonna have some fun," she said. "All three of us."

Raider was agreeable.

"Ain't it good to have friends?" Rosey offered.

"It sure is," the big man replied, forgetting his miseries. "It sure as hell is."